DATE DUE

OCT 2 3 1996	
NOV 0 4 1996	
NOV 2 8 1996	
JUL 1 1 1997	
JUL 1 4 1997	

HOW A
PEOPLE
DIE

A novel by
ALAN FRY

with an introduction
and an afterword
by the author

HARBOUR PUBLISHING

Copyright ©1994 by Alan Fry
Original edition published by Doubleday & Company,
   Toronto & New York, copyright ©1970 by Alan Fry

Harbour Publishing
P.O. Box 219
Madeira Park, BC Canada V0N 2H0

Cover design by Roger Handling
Cover photograph *Weeping Woman Totem, Kispiox* by Anne
   Cameron

Canadian Cataloguing in Publication Data

Fry, Alan, 1931–
   How a people die

ISBN 1-55017-106-2

1. Indians of North America—Canada, Western—Fiction.
   I. Title.
PS8511.R88H6 1994   C813'.54   C94-910485-X
PR9199.3.F79H6 1994

To my mother, who knows about hard work

CONTENTS

INTRODUCTION

W hen *How a People Die* was first published I was often asked why I had decided to speak out. The book put my job in the federal Indian service at risk and certainly would offend many Indian people, though not all by any means. Since one doesn't get rich writing this sort of book, why did I do it?

The answer lay in my acute frustration at the reluctance of us all—field workers, Indian leaders, department officials at headquarters, politicians—to talk about the real guts of what it was like in the villages where the people lived—and so often died on account of how they lived.

We administered social assistance, we operated schools and sent children to school, we built houses and, where money and terrain allowed, installed piped water and sewage disposal. We worked with band councils to administer timber, grazing, gravel and other natural resources on reserve lands. We administered the land itself for internal use by the people or through leasing to outsiders for revenue for band funds. Contrary to popular myth, we worked with Indian leadership in most of what we did.

But little of what we did, or even talked about, directly addressed the harsh reality of daily life in the villages—widespread heavy drinking, brutal violence against women and children by husbands, fathers and other men, sexual abuse including considerable incest, dreadful neglect of children.

The silence of the Indian leaders was in some measure understandable. Those who had some talent to lead and who had accepted responsibility for their people were overwhelmed by what they had undertaken. They could deal with the practical difficulties of schools, houses, water systems and resource use. What could they do about the rest of it—the drinking, the beating, the incest, the child neglect?

Particularly what could they do about it when, as was so often the case, some of these horrific behaviours affected their own families, affected themselves?

A majority of the leaders were men and men dominated life in Indian villages, notwithstanding an ostensible respect for prominent women. If these men did not themselves practice the abhorrent behaviours, they most often had male kin who did, male kin against whom they found it impossible to speak, let alone take action.

They did not want to talk about the drinking, the beating, the incest and the child neglect. Senior people in the department, the politicians and an articulate but ignorant segment of the public, imbued with romantic notions, hardly wanted to know about, much less discuss, these harsh realities.

So I decided that I would talk, as best I could with my limited talent, and *How a People Die* got written and published.

A considerable fuss followed.

A few Indian leaders outside my district demanded that I be fired. Senior officials in the department remained surprisingly calm, however, in what I believe was a tacit acknowledgment that perhaps it was no bad thing to call a spade a spade so long as they hadn't done it and couldn't be held responsible. In the broader community the book attracted a good deal of attention, much of it predictable, and some quite gratifying. Reviews of the book appeared in the press all over Canada and the United States, for the most part overwhelmingly positive.

The Indian leaders in my own district soon sent word to Indian politicians elsewhere to back off, they would deal with me as they saw fit. I had enjoyed an open and forthright relationship with the band councils in my district and they now made clear that my future in the service was their business only. I appreciated enormously their firm stand against pressure from outside the district, and I put to them the position I had known all along I would feel compelled to adopt: I would accept their decision, I would continue to work with them in the same forthright way I always had or I would quit the service.

A meeting of chiefs and a number of leading council members convened of an evening at the district office. Speeches were made and harsh words said but more, I sensed, for appearances necessary to band and tribal politics than because I had done anything truly outrageous. After all the formal speeches were given I left the meeting and the chiefs and councilors got down to the closed-door discussion necessary to a decision.

In the upshot I stayed and over the days that followed several of the chiefs, in the privacy of my office, conveyed their understanding for what I had done. Implicit, of course, was that I must also understand the necessity of their public position. I thought it an abundantly fair exchange.

(I did, in fact, resign from the service four years later but not from any frustration in working with Indian leadership, however much I wished the chiefs and their councils would more directly face the reality of alcohol-related violence in their villages. When the end came, it grew out of immense frustration with government bureaucracy and the inconsistency between departmental objectives and what might best be done with federal funds in the villages. But that is another long story.)

One of the bands in my district was widely known for its success in adapting to mainstream economic and social conditions. Many of the men in the village were successful seine-boat skippers, earning substantial incomes and putting their money to good use. Most families maintained a standard of living which many who perceive themselves secure in the Canadian middle class well might envy.

It was during this time that I asked the chief of this band to go with one of my field officers to see first hand the real life village that was the Kwatsi in *How a People Die*. The two bands had little in common and the chief of the progressive village had never visited the other. He readily agreed.

After the trip, this chief came to my office to express his

horror at what he had seen and his sympathy for my field staff in trying to achieve anything in such a place. It had been beyond his belief that any people could be so hopelessly incapable of doing something for themselves or of making constructive use of the help extended by government. He did not condemn but neither could he understand.

I recall his words: "It's far worse than you made it in your book."

Yet many asked then, is it really that bad?

Many ask now, is it really that bad?

In writing then I used the death statistics of an actual community to demonstrate how bad it was and to say, further, that if you tell us how a people die, we can tell you how a people live.

How bad is it?

I will provide more recent death and other statistics which demonstrate that, indeed, the situation remains persistently desperate.

But first let me give more life to what these numbers mean. The following statements included in the report of the Canadian Panel on Violence Against Women bring to life the brutality behind the numbers:

> My father used to beat my mother all the time. When we were young I would hear them coming down the path toward the house after being out drinking. I could hear him yelling and him hitting her. The next day we would go to school and the blood of my mother could be seen on the snow bank and her hair on the road.

> Gang rapes happen, on and off reserve, white men and Aboriginal men, young women and old women. A young girl was at a party, her stepfather and her uncle raped her in front of a friend and some young boys. They stuffed her mouth with pills to try and kill her to prevent her from telling. The friend and the young boys tried to stop it from happening. When the friend told the community social services worker what had happened, the community told the girl it was her fault that she got raped because she went to the party. She pressed charges and the judge asked her if she wanted to continue. The stepfather killed himself, and

then it came out that there was incest all through the family over generations.

A friend of mine had foster daughters. She found out her husband had been raping them for years. He was sentenced to ninety days. There was no appeal from the Crown attorney.

By the time I was ten years old I was raped four times. Nothing was done for me.

I was gang-raped at two and a half years of age by a grown man, his brothers and friends. My brother assaulted me until the police intervened and then my grandfather started. I remember them raping me and putting a diaper on me and the diaper filling with blood. They broke my feet, and I remember being put in a room and them coming in to give me suckers. Why did my family do this to me?

There have been gang rapes of teenagers. They're afraid to mention it. One was reported, but charges were withdrawn because the victim was scared. There were two gang rapes last year, in a house in which drinking goes on. One girl refused to go back to her foster home. The three guys that did it, nothing happened to them. They get the girls drunk and use them, have sex with them. They use drinking as an excuse.

I was abused by my parents who were alcoholics. I was sexually abused. I was abused in foster care. I went back to the reserve to be sexually abused by siblings. My daughter was gang-raped at a party when she was sixteen. It is almost normal in this area.

Credible statements and reports from Indian women's associations make clear that violence against women and children is widespread throughout reserve communities.

Information revealed in recent enquiries and studies provides a vivid image of this truly dreadful violence.

From the Report of the Aboriginal Justice Inquiry of Manitoba, Hamilton and Sinclair, 1991:

Presentations of Aboriginal women were blunt and direct. Violence and abuse in Aboriginal communities has reached epidemic proportions. This violence takes a number of forms. Sometimes it involves physical assaults between adult males. More often—and more disturbingly—it involves the victimization of the least powerful members of the community: women and children.

From the Fatality Inquiries Act Report Respecting the Death of Lester Norman Desjarlais, Associate Chief Judge Brian Dale Giesbrecht, 1992:

The sexual abuse of children is a horror of our time. Lester was only one of a depressingly large number of children who are used like meat by their elders for sexual purposes and then cast aside with their childhoods in shreds.

Problems associated with dysfunctionalism, such as alcohol abuse, child abuse and violence are far more extensive and intractable in reserve communities than in non-Aboriginal communities.

... the evidence is overwhelming that the social problems on Indian reserves are grossly out of proportion to those in the nation at large ...

From *A New Justice for Indian Children: Final Report of the Child Advocacy Project*, Longstaffe & Hamilton, Children's Hospital Child Protection Centre, Winnipeg, 1987:

The problem of child sexual assault is one that has reached epidemic proportions in recent years. Due to the rapid rise in reported instances of child sexual abuse, demand for knowledge on the subject far exceeds supply.

Children (on Indian reserves in Manitoba) are suffering from trauma, physical injury, and psychological devastation that result from sexual abuse. The injuries to self-esteem, trust, and emotional functioning last a lifetime. The incidence of sniffing, alcohol abuse, eating disorders, suicide, depression, and sexual acting out among Indian children suggest that the problem of child sexual abuse has reached epidemic proportions.

From *Breaking Free: A Proposal for Change to Aboriginal Family Violence*, Ontario Women's Association, 1989:

> . . . 84% of respondents indicated that family violence occurs in their communities . . .

> . . . 80% of respondents indicated they had personally experienced family violence.

> . . . the incidence of family violence in Aboriginal communities is eight times higher than the average for Canadian society as a whole.

> . . . 87% of respondents indicated that physical abuse was a feature (of family violence) . . .

> . . . 57% of respondents suggested that sexual abuse was a feature of family violence in Aboriginal communities.

> The batterer was identified as the husband with an incidence of 84% . . .

> . . . nearly 24% of surveyed individuals indicated they personally know cases of family violence which had led to death—most frequently, to the women.

Into this already perilous mix now comes the human immunodeficiency virus, HIV, linked to the deadly disease we call acquired immune deficiency syndrome or AIDS. Given the extensive and indiscriminate sexual activity now common in Indian communities, much of it in drunkenness and much of it by force, a deadly epidemic is virtually certain. Entire villages could be all but wiped out.

Here are some numbers.

A report from Health and Welfare Canada for 1990, *Health Status of Canadian Indians and Inuit*, discloses that between 1984 and 1988, the death rate for the registered Indian population served in the ages fifteen through forty-five was three and a half times the Canadian average.

Yet another report, this by Indian and Northern Affairs entitled *Highlights of Aboriginal Conditions: Part II: Social Conditions,* tells us that in 1976 the overall rate of violent deaths for status Indians was more than three times the national average, that in 1981 it was over four times the national rate, and that by 1986 it was just under three times the national rate. A more recent Health and Welfare Canada report suggests it may really be as high as ten times the non-Indian average.

Crime statistics also suggest that life continues to be harsh and tragic for inordinate numbers of Indian people.

According to a 1988 report by the Solicitor General of Canada, although Aboriginal people represent only 2% of Canada's population, they represent 10% of the nation's federal penitentiary population.

A 1993 report by the Canadian Centre for Justice asserts that the situation is not improving, citing the case of Regina in 1990 where Aboriginal persons, while comprising only 5% of the population, comprised 43% of those accused of criminal offenses. Further, the crime rate for Aboriginal persons was found to be more than twelve times that of non-Aboriginal persons.

Other comparisons from this report are revealing: while Aboriginal persons comprised only 5% of the total Regina population in 1990, they comprised 31% of the victims of violent crime.

The largest proportion of Aboriginal victims were spouses or ex-spouses (24%); further, 28% of all Aboriginal victims were living with the accused.

The violence pictured in Regina is not unique to the urban situations in which many Indians now live.

Cruel new dimensions have been added to the violence in Indian villages in recent years: gas sniffing and suicide, mainly by young adults, adolescents and children, with sexual abuse emerging as a common ingredient in the early experience of those who take up sniffing and the many who go on from sniffing to end their lives.

In the report Health Status of Canadian Indians and Inuit, we find that the suicide rate for registered Indian boys served by Medical Services of National Health & Welfare (primarily status Indians on reserves or in crown land settlements) between the ages of ten and fourteen years is seven times that of the same age group in the general Canadian population. For Indian girls in the age group, the rate is thirteen times the rate of that age group in the general population. In the age group from fifteen to nineteen, Indian male adolescents commit suicide at five times the national rate; Indian female adolescents at six times the national rate.

What can be done about the frightening complex of alcoholism, violence and death on the reserves is anything but clear. Different panaceas have been popular at different times. I recall when education was declared, ad nauseum, to be the key. Repeatedly, new federal ministers have announced new programs by which, once and for all, housing conditions were to be brought to a decent standard. Brave new programs in economic development emerge from time to time.

The commitment in financial terms has been significant. Federal expenditures on Aboriginal programs have grown from 2.1% of overall federal expenditures (excluding expenditures on public debt) in 1975-76 to 4.2% in 1992-93. In per capita terms, this spending is now in the order of $12,400 for each status Indian living on-reserve or in a crown land settlement.

Now we hear much of the inherent right to self-government, of the need for separate Aboriginal justice systems, of how we must settle outstanding land claims, of the need for Indians to take charge of their own education and welfare, of how everything will come right when First Nations have control of their own destiny.

With qualification, I sympathize with much of the change being proposed, but I am skeptical of the assumption it will coincidentally purge the myriad social ills that plague aboriginal communities.

II

Once, long ago, in the cold mists of a summer dawn, I hauled a man off the woman he was beating in the mud and slime of a road-side ditch on a violence-plagued reserve where I lived, in some anxiety, with my own young family. I held him off by force with one arm while I fetched the bleeding woman to her feet with the other. His whiskey-laden breath betrayed a night at least and perhaps several days of heavy drinking. Bloody booze again, I thought, but the dreadful vulnerability of Indian people to alcohol had been anchored in my mind for most of thirty years, even then, and that was thirty-five years ago.

To more fully understand my perspective on alcohol and its role in the problems of aboriginal people, which has only become more set since writing *How A People Die*, it may be helpful to know some personal background.

I grew up among native people in rural BC, although my family was recently transplanted from quite different circumstances.

I descend from founding Quakers who farmed in the seventeenth century in Wiltshire but my grandfather, Roger Fry, descending more immediately from the chocolate Frys, graduated from Cambridge and kept company in the much-celebrated Bloomsbury Group, where he was known for his writings on art. My father set out for British Columbia at least in part to escape the fame which Roger then enjoyed—in England he might never be other than Roger's son.

Compared to my father's, my own early life appears as a leap backward in time. I grew up in pioneer Cariboo ranch country where my most memorable nights were spent around campfires flickering on a circle of mostly aboriginal faces—a world away, and a century as well, from the lamp-lit halls of King's College and Vanessa Bell's much-decorated living room at Charleston.

Life was hard, perhaps. We worked twelve-hour days, seven days a week in the heavy labour of harvest alongside mixed-ancestry natives with here and there a full blood. Little cash circulated in the rural economy.

People today can have little sense of how different life was then. A woman of mixed ancestry who contributed greatly to my early years—genetically she was mostly Aboriginal but she lacked status—told of hunting hare with her brother using a muzzle-loading gun, of catching a ride on a freight wagon to travel between communities on the Cariboo Road.

As recently as the thirties, most Canadians and virtually all Aboriginal Canadians lived in rural and mainly isolated regions. In much of rural Canada, those were the last years of the frontier condition, much more akin to the century before than any time since. Among white and Indian alike, families and the old were cared for and the beliefs and values which enforce the basic decencies that all people must observe if they are to live together in gentleness still prevailed.

This is the way I understand the true character of aboriginal people, not the way I knew it as an Indian Affairs employee struggling to help the unhappy community I have called Kwatsi in *How A People Die*, or in the picture that emerges from today's headlines about child suicide pacts on northern reserves. In government service it was all too easy for some to believe that the massive dysfunction confronting one daily was an inherent condition of native existence with deep historical roots beyond the poor power of any individual to change, justifying an attitude of resigned acceptance. I was never afforded that luxury, because I was too conscious of how much better aboriginal existence had been as recently as my own youth.

There had been many changes in non-aboriginal life too, but nothing like the precipice native communities had gone over between the beginning of WWII and 1970 when *How A People Die* was published. There are many influences which could account for such a sharp deterioration in the quality of aboriginal life, but it seems appropriate to begin by asking if there was any obvious factor differentiating those two eras which might account for the striking abruptness of that change.

As it happens, such a factor does exist: alcohol.

Before the Second World War alcohol was consumed, surreptitiously, only by a persistent few who lived within convenient reach of bootleggers. The great majority of the people had no ready access to alcohol and although life was not easy, it had some order to it. Sexual abuse no doubt existed, but my own experience makes me think it was of an altogether lesser order. When I was five an adolescent aboriginal boy tried to persuade me to masturbate him. We were in bush land in the ranch country of my boyhood, some distance from both the ranch house in which I lived and the brush camp in which he lived. We had come on a magnificent paper wasp nest, deserted but intact. He took it down from the branch and I desperately wanted it to take home. He offered it but the price was that I should fondle his penis. I would not and he held the nest just out of my reach in inducement. The persuasion went on for some time. He continued to offer the valued nest for the indicated price which, badly though I wanted the nest, I would not pay. Finally I went home without the nest and he without satisfaction but not once was there a hint of violence. He came from a family in which the essential values were yet intact. Two generations later in that same family, after alcohol had done its work, few adolescent or grown men would have hesitated to abuse a child by physical force to get an orgasm.

It is my firm conviction that the succession of increasingly destructive lifestyles can be traced back to the end of liquor prohibition to status Indians in the decade following the Second World War.

A general prosperity, coupled with expansion of the cash economy in the rural and isolated parts of the country after the war, together with changes in the law meant, suddenly, that Indians everywhere could buy and consume alcohol freely, with tragic results. However you want to account for it, a majority of Indian people were devastatingly vulnerable to alcohol. For many, family and community life began to unravel.

The children born in the sixties are in or approaching their thirties now. For many, the tragedy continues. Born to drinking parents, they now drink. The argument is widely advanced that this generation of parents, the last to attend the residential schools, do not know how to parent because they spent so much time in the schools. I won't defend the residential schools because too much went wrong there but I do argue that the heavy drinking in their parents' generation which continues in their own is far more responsible than the residential schools for the dreadful neglect of today's children.

The Health and Welfare Canada report referred to earlier, *Health Status of Canadian Indians and Inuit (1990)*, discloses that the elevated death rate for the registered Indian population in the ages fifteen through forty-five was due in seventy-five per cent of cases to "injury and poisoning". The report is remarkable in avoiding any explanation of the nature of the injuries or of the poisonings, but separately a Solicitor General of Canada and Attorney General of Alberta report (1991) found that in most

Aboriginal communities at least 80% of the people had alcohol problems.

The Ontario Women's Association study "Breaking Free: A Proposal for Change to Aboriginal Family Violence," recorded that:

> 44% of respondents said alcohol was often involved and 37% said it was usually found in a violent situation.
>
> The finding is corroborated by an earlier study of Aboriginal women in Nova Scotia which suggested that in 90% of the cases of family violence, women indicated that alcohol abuse was the immediate cause of the problem.
>
> Of the respondents to our survey, alcoholism was identified as a main cause of family violence by 78% of the respondents. (15% said they did not know and only 6% said no.)

The report assumes that alcohol is not the cause of family violence, preferring to attribute it to pressures on the Indian community by the wider society, and reports that:

> All but one of the respondents said alcohol was associated with family violence yet most recognized that it was not the cause.

However, the report includes a recommendation that:

> The level of services required . . . to treat and combat the abuse of alcohol, drugs, and solvents, must be immediately increased in order to address a problem intimately connected to the high incidence of family violence . . .

In the 1993 report by the Canadian Centre for Justice cited earlier, 38% of Regina Aboriginals accused of violent crimes were reported to have used alcohol and/or drugs compared to 23% of non-Aboriginals accused; 30% of Aboriginal victims used alcohol and/or drugs compared to 11% of non-Aboriginal victims.

It has been for a long time conventional wisdom that the high rates of alcohol dependence among Indians are the consequence of bad treatment by the dominant culture.

A variety of ills are cited and said to be the problem: segregation on reserves, the residential school experience, lack of economic opportunity, the vagaries of an alien justice system, poor housing, lack of running water and modern sewage disposal, dependence created by government hand-outs, the general assault on native culture by the wider society.

In this view, aboriginal people drink because they have and continue to be treated badly.

Certainly the people have been treated badly, though not always and often without intent. Much of the time, there has been more ineptitude than malevolence.

But to see the illness of alcoholism as a consequence of this treatment is to miss the reality that the disease is, in fact, the root cause of most that is now wrong in Indian communities.

Not having a sufficient or regular income is indeed a hardship but it does not lead inevitably to squalor and violence, to wife beating and sexual abuse of children, to appallingly high accidental death rates.

Critics of government treatment of Indians assert that inferior housing is a prime reason for the drinking which afflicts so many Indian communities, but response to the very houses provided under subsidy programs perfectly belies the argument: provided to a non-drinking family wanting to make the most of them, these houses can be clean, warm and cheerful; occupied by a family in which one or more key members are alcoholic, more often than not they are soon reduced to a squalid, stinking shambles.

Few families in the community of my boyhood had more than rudimentary housing. Some lived in one or two-room cabins, using tents and other outbuildings to provide additional sleeping space. Indoor toilets and running water were exceedingly scarce. One large family moved about frequently while contracting harvest work on the cattle ranches. These people cleaned up then lived in the humblest cabins imaginable, on one occasion sweeping the manure out of an old horse barn to make it livable. They used canvas liberally, particularly in summer, and once I stayed with them in a one-room cabin, hastily built of green unbarked logs with sod heaped on stout poles for a roof and hard-packed earth for a floor. Although it was winter, a separate tent provided space for cooking and eating.

If small, cramped quarters and a lack of indoor plumbing lead to alcoholism then this family and most of the community of my boyhood should have suffered the most widespread alcoholic drinking you could imagine. But just the opposite was the case.

The heavy, destructive drinking of the manifest alcoholic all but guarantees a lifestyle of the most brutal poverty imaginable and will do so irrespective of economic opportunity or of any other ingredient of social fairness. Of course, alcoholic drinking has led to this same brutal poverty in countless non-Indian families as well. The particular tragedy for Indian communities lies in the exceptionally high incidence of alcoholism among people of Aboriginal and mixed ancestry, with the disease at times afflicting entire settlements.

So what is the nature of this disease?

I do have some personal insight because I am myself an alcoholic and I've had to deal with that reality.

In the experience of countless alcoholics, myself very much included, the alcoholic is born not made.

The alcoholic comes into the world carrying the factor for alcoholism, whatever that factor may be. For years this was widely believed by common folk though staunchly repudiated in authoritative circles. Now such a prestigious institution as the U.S. National Institute on Drug Abuse is emboldened to say that "research findings suggest genetic factors are involved in the etiology of alcoholism" and that "research has strongly implicated a role for genetic factors."

All that is necessary to develop from a latent to a manifest alcoholic, with a full case of destructive drinking that is characteristic of the alcoholic, is exposure to alcohol.

The exposure required varies: some alcoholics are in major trouble on the first drink, others may appear to be moderate drinkers for years before the disease becomes evident. This was so in my case. The disease crept up on me through apparently safe social drinking which led to a powerful addiction. Fortunately I did not develop violent behaviours and I was fairly adept at keeping the dependency a secret from most people outside my immediate family and close associates, but the alcoholism is every bit as real for all of that.

Alcoholics do not drink because they have problems, although they do have problems because they drink. Indeed, the abundance of their problems often convinces both the alcoholic and others sympathetic to his/her cause, that the problems are the cause of the drinking. The alcoholic says if you had my problems, you'd drink, too; the sympathizer says it's too bad John drinks but if I had his problems, I'd probably drink, too. Neither of them knows what they are talking about, although if he is fortunate enough to get into recovery, the alcoholic may eventually get it right.

This is not to say, of course, that alcoholics may not have problems other than those they have brought on themselves with their drinking. Indeed they often do and such problems are also very handy to cite as further reason for the drinking.

Many alcoholics were abused as children. Also, alcoholics do not like to accept responsibility for their drinking. How convenient it is then to say you drink because you were abused as a child, especially if well meaning people with no experience of alcoholism will then rally with sympathy to your cause.

If you are an alcoholic of mixed ancestry who attended a residential school, the chances are you did not have a happy time there. Deplorably, you may have been abused sexually. It will be very easy for you to believe that the residential school experience is why you drink.

The reality, however, points in a different direction. Large numbers of people with sexual and general abuse in their childhoods are not alcoholics. Also, many people without significant trauma in their childhoods are alcoholics. Bad circumstances do not make people into alcoholics. Alcoholism is inherent in the individual, not in his or her circumstances. All he or she needs is exposure to alcohol to proceed, sooner or later, to destructive drinking.

Unfortunately, the only way to discover whether or not you are an alcoholic is to drink and by the time you have the answer, if it is affirmative, it is already too late. The only hope left then is recovery through not drinking, keeping in mind that recovery is only from destructive, alcoholic drinking. There is no cure for the disease itself. One drink can be enough to take the alcoholic in recovery back to full-scale, destructive drinking.

It was not without good intentions that the Parliament of

Canada, for many decades, made it illegal to supply Indians with alcohol and for Indians to consume alcohol. From the earliest days of European occupation it had been obvious that the great majority of Indian people, including people of significant Aboriginal content in mixed ancestry, were in major trouble if they drank at all. Unscrupulous traders took advantage of this affliction, without mercy and for great material gain.

After the appearance of *How A People Die*, I was branded a racist for merely implying that alcoholism is an inheritable disease and that Indian people inherit it to a greater extent than do non-Indians. But I do not argue that Indian people are inferior because of this, only that they carry an added and dreadfully unfortunate burden, just as blacks are recognized by science to carry the gene for sickle-cell anemia. I don't perceive that I am inferior because I happen to be an alcoholic. Why would I extend the notion of inferiority to a whole race of people because they suffer a high rate of this disease?

At any rate, discriminatory and paternalistic it may have been but in many regions of Canada, this prohibition based on race helped substantially. Communities in more isolated locations, beyond practical reach of bootleggers, were largely free of alcohol. People were not prosperous but an economy based on trapping, fishing and hunting and supplemented by such occupations as occasional guiding, logging or cattle raising, depending on opportunity, provided important self-reliance. Tuberculosis was by any reckoning the greater threat and took more lives until modern drugs turned the tide after the Second World War.

The prohibition on alcohol could not be continued but a dreadful price was paid on its passing. Thousands of people who had lived modestly productive lives in stable communities became manifest alcoholics, descending into the violently abusive poverty which follows on constant, heavy drinking.

A few communities have made their own decision to return to prohibition, with mixed success. Old Crow, in the northern Yukon Territory, was a remarkably self-reliant community with little strife before alcohol became easily available during the nineteen-sixties. Since then, the people have endured a painful time of violence, crime and untimely death. Now, the stronger among them struggle to lead their community back to health, hoping that prohibition will achieve a critical advantage.

Many native leaders and other Canadians want to believe that redress of outstanding treaty grievances, land claim settlements where these have yet to be achieved, self-government (whatever, ultimately, that will entail), more education and training, and improved economic opportunity generally will lead the inordinately large number of people now caught up in alcoholic poverty out of their despair and into a new life of sobriety and peaceful living.

These ambitions are worthy in their own right, but any hope that their achievement will solve the alcohol problem is founded on a failure to understand the nature of the disease. There will be much disappointment at the end of the day.

No alcoholic will ever be brought into recovery because someone else settles the ancestral grievances of his people, gives him a good house with full plumbing and electricity, provides him more education, gets him a steady job or arranges matters so that his people will enjoy self-government.

Alcoholics come into recovery as a result of personal decision: there comes a time when fear of what is happening in their lives leads them to look for a way out. A desperate need to escape the addiction begins to compete with the desperate need for alcohol. They are ready then to be helped and they may make the break for freedom. Their chances will be greater if useful supports are then available.

Many succeed; considerably more do not.

It is, however, in the words of many an alcoholic in recovery, an inside job.

Now, with all that said, it will still be argued that where people have no economic opportunity whatever, where whole communities are reduced to beggary, surely alcoholic drinking must prevail, surely even the most resolute among us will eventually lose hope and turn to the bottle or some equivalent.

The dependent community is not new in human experience. Life may not be easy in such places but it will be better or worse according to how people deal with it.

Repeatedly over millennia groups of people have lost their economic base; they have had either to devise new means of generating wealth, to move on, to perish, or to depend on wealth generated elsewhere being transferred to their community. Whole nations in our time depend on transfers of wealth, often in the form of food aid, to stay alive.

Aboriginal communities in what is now Canada lived where animals, fish and useful plants afforded sufficient resources for survival in a stone-age economy. Many of today's First Nations communities remain at these sites, useful in Aboriginal times but frequently affording little access to the mainstream economy of the late twentieth century.

Still, people whose Aboriginal ancestors expected to live entirely by the land, to eat captured and gathered food, to live in brush shelters and wear skin clothing, now reasonably expect to live in houses, wear textile clothing, eat some range of store foods, use basic household appliances, own a useful vehicle (boat and motor, skidoo, light truck perhaps), listen to a radio, watch a television set and generally consume the sorts of goods most other Canadians consume.

In the highly interdependent world in which we live, economic independence at best means that during what ought to be our employable years we can earn enough income through employment or entrepreneurship to buy what we need for a level of consumption that at least approaches the average of the wider community.

The sites of many northern or otherwise remote Indian communities, useful in Aboriginal times or selected for their advantages during the better years of the fur trade, are not now economically viable. The majority of those who live there cannot earn enough money to maintain anything like the standard of living most Canadians are conditioned to expect.

To varying degrees, these are dependent communities: communities in which personal and family incomes depend heavily on government expenditures. A few government jobs requiring minimal skills—cleaning up at the school or the nursing station, for example—together with government funded social assistance programs, provide the bulk of cash income to people of normally employable age.

This is not exclusively a First Nations experience. Many non-Indian communities, in the Atlantic provinces, for example, where the economic base has crumbled, face the same dependence on wealth transferred in by way of government support programs.

(In a somewhat different but related way, the whole of the Yukon Territory is largely a dependent community, though the dependence is disguised through a disproportionate level of federally funded public sector employment. Notwithstanding some mining and tourism, the economy is largely underpinned by federal transfers to the Government of Yukon together with direct federal program expenditures. In 1994, these amounted to almost $14,500 per capita annually, which works out to just under $58,500 for every family of four. Communities underpinned by social assistance aren't so affluent, though the source of wealth is the same—the Canadian taxpayer.)

On the face of it, dependence by a remote First Nations community on minor government employment and considerable social assistance should not have to be a disastrous arrangement. If the location still affords the opportunity to hunt, fish, and gather wood for fuel and if the people are disposed to use their time to get the most they can from the land, the limited cash, topped up perhaps with some trapping or craft income, may round out a reasonable living.

Many families have, in fact, succeeded at this mixed livelihood and entire communities have done well at it. The longer term implications, given a growing population and no new economic opportunity in sight, may be worrying, but as a way of life for today, it beats a city slum by a country mile.

But if on the face of it this arrangement does not have to be disastrous, dropping alcohol into the mix guarantees a disaster in spades.

Time that would have been spent on the land is then spent drinking or being sick from having been drinking. Cash that would have gone to fuel for the outboard motor or skidoo or to a little store food to go with the land food or to any of a number of modest needs which make life on the land productive, then goes to alcohol.

And the violence begins.

Let there be no mistake on this point: it is not the mix of social assistance with living off the land which leads to the alcoholic drinking. It is the alcoholic drinking which destroys the will to make use of this limited though workable way of life.

The wider Canadian community should be concerned about the continuing growth of dependent communities in regions where economic opportunity obliges people to rely on wealth transferred in from elsewhere. The future of these communities is indeed precarious.

At the same time, we need to be clear that today's grief in these communities is a direct consequence of heavy, alcoholic drinking, not of restricted economic opportunity.

If alcoholic drinking with all its consequences could be set aside, the life experience of Indian people in Canada would be at least as promising as that of other average citizens. To the extent that Indian leaders, governments and other Canadians want to address the misery which afflicts so many of these people, they must face, directly, the problem of alcoholic drinking.

Let me say again: directly. There are no indirect approaches of any use whatever: you can't deal with alcoholic drinking by building houses or installing indoor plumbing. These may have merit in their own right but they will do nothing to alleviate alcoholic drinking.

Neither is this a problem which can be tackled without the active participation of the alcoholics who are doing the drinking. An individual will stop drinking only by accepting responsibility for his or her own behaviour and making necessary change; a community will recover from the destructive effects of alcoholic drinking only to the extent that individuals within the community make essential changes in their own lives. Community recovery is no more nor less than the accumulation of individual recovery.

At the heart of recovery is the acceptance of responsibility.

So what is government to do?

Perhaps the most instructive experience of any community in recent years is that of the Alkali Lake Band in the Chilcotin country southwest of Williams Lake in British Columbia. This band had suffered dreadful alcoholism and brutal violence, beginning mainly in the years following the second war. Still, from the initiative largely of Phyllis and Andy Chelsea, a couple who managed to break from their own drinking and then to help others, the community has become almost entirely sober and greatly recovered from not only the drinking but the painful and deadly violence which stemmed from it. A key factor has been the vigorously determined leadership of Andy following his election as chief, a powerful illustration of the importance of Aboriginal leaders committing themselves to the task of community recovery.

The Alkali Lake story was told in a film produced by the community entitled *The Honour of All—the Alkali Lake Story* which has been seen widely throughout North America. Also, publications available in most libraries contain accounts of the achievement. Here I will quote from *The Path to Healing—Report of the National Round Table on Aboriginal Health and Social Issues* (1993—Vancouver, BC) to illustrate key principles in this recovery experience:

> The problem that must be addressed is the disease of alcoholism. It is a disease that is medically recognized as having no cure; it can only be controlled through abstinence.
>
> Based on the historical study of the interventions used at Alkali Lake between 1972 and the present and the data gathered in the 1992 research, several conclusions emerge:
>
> 1. The confrontation intervention was used to get people to stop drinking. The key elements of this method are the provision of choices, expressions of concern and follow-through on the ultimatum. Using the steps correctly results in the ultimatum not appearing as force, and people feel they have made the choice themselves.
>
> 2. After-care. The treatment alone is not sufficient to maintain sobriety. Many aspects of after-care must be developed to facilitate a healing process. Without after-care the risk of relapse is high . . .
>
> 3. Training in alcoholism and how to work effectively with alcoholic clients. The research submits that the alcoholic client and the alcoholic community do not constitute a hopeless situation but can respond to a combination of sober leadership, structured interventions, and resources for healing and after-care.

4. Family Support. The statistics show that family was the biggest factor in people's decision to quit drinking.

5. Spiritual Support. . . . it can be concluded that . . . specific planned intervention to revive and relearn Aboriginal spiritual ceremonies played a significant and substantial role in the recovery of the Alkali Lake community.

It is paramount in the Alkali Lake achievement that the disease of alcoholism was recognized to be the cause of the community's grief, and that individuals in the community accepted responsibility for their own behaviour and recovery. These people then worked with others to extend the recovery throughout the community.

Turning to the problem of destructive alcoholic drinking in First Nations communities at large, the time has come to spell out clearly that primary responsibility for recovery lies with the people themselves. Past injustice is not the issue. Recovery is the issue and recovery is available only to those who accept responsibility.

Residential treatment for detoxification, intensive support following detoxification (in residence when necessary) and longer term counseling should be offered. Where these are available, individuals taking action for their own recovery have the best chance of success.

These programs do not need elaborate physical facilities nor expensive staff. Well trained counselors and basic accommodation will do.

The Alcoholics Anonymous (AA) program achieves a significant rate of recovery in meeting rooms of the most ordinary sort, with all costs met from contributions by the participating alcoholics.

All counselors should be aware of how the AA program works. Volunteers can be asked to visit to explain how an AA group can be established in a community seeking recovery.

Where community leaders wish to establish treatment programs but do not have the money, government should provide the funds, with firm conditions attached.

First, only basic physical facilities should be provided. This trip calls for economy, not first class. Expensive facilities add nothing to recovery.

Second, the treatment program must be well defined before funds are advanced.

Third, the counseling philosophy must be based on acceptance by the alcoholic of personal responsibility for present behaviour and for recovery. **Only counseling which persistently advances the concept of personal responsibility should be supported.**

Fourth, counselors working in alcohol addiction must focus on how to break from and to gain the strength to remain free from drinking. Other problems consequent on the drinking will be resolved by addressing the drinking; problems not related to the drinking must be referred elsewhere. Alcohol workers who take on the other problems of the alcoholic are no longer working on the alcohol problem.

The job of the alcohol counselor is to carry to the alcoholic the message of recovery through accepting personal responsibility, not to carry the alcoholic.

No funds should be provided to any community on a do-your-own-thing, no-conditions-attached basis.

At the same time that it promotes and supports an attack on alcoholic drinking, an attack in which Aboriginal leaders must be fully involved, the federal government, with the co-operation of the provinces, the territories and Aboriginal leadership, must bring to public view the serious extent of violence, including sexual violence, against women and children in First Nations communities.

While the attack on alcoholic drinking is the long term solution for the bulk of this violence, exposure of its nature and extent with an immediate increase in protection for women and children is mandatory.

Those who wish to link this issue with historic grievances may do so for whatever purpose it may serve them: the women and children will be served only by governments, including Aboriginal governments, fully exposing the extent of their suffering and taking action at all levels to control it.

Put bluntly, all the injustice done by the wider Canadian community to the people of mixed heritage we call Aboriginal—and that injustice has been at times both grievous and enormous—does not excuse, nor indeed explain, the brutal treatment of so many women and children by their men.

Again, the time has arrived for plain speaking, for acknowledging that nursing historic grievances is not how to deal with today's persistent violence against women and children.

It is time for leaders in First Nations communities to face this problem head on but if any do not wish to do so, the federal, provincial and territorial governments must in any case take action.

Above all, as the federal government moves to give expression to what has been called the inherent right to self-government, no provision must be allowed which will cause women and children in Aboriginal communities to have less protection from violence than is provided to other citizens in the wider community. Indian women's groups have expressed great worry about self-government being enshrined in the Constitution: with first hand knowledge of how little protection they now have in male-dominated communities, they fear a self-government formula which will leave them without recourse from the attitudes and practices of the men who dominate the band councils where they live.

Indian self-government must not be so structured that women and children living under such a government have less protection than is afforded to other Canadian citizens by other levels of government.

III

Except to consider their possible implications for addressing alcoholic drinking and its consequent violence, and improving the lot of Indian women and children, the complex issues of Aboriginal rights, land claims and the inherent right to self-government, of which we hear much these days, lie largely beyond the scope of this discussion.

Obviously, before the arrival of the Europeans and before the history of French or British North American began, the Aboriginal people, living sometimes in small, scattered bands and at other times in larger tribal groups, governed themselves.

Their descendants today, through the leadership of the bands recognized under the Indian Act and through various other Aboriginal organizations, some of which include non-status Indians and Metis, argue an inherent right to self-government, a right never extinguished, neither by treaty nor by conquest. The federal government, with the support of some territorial and provincial governments, now concedes the point.

In fact, Indian bands do now exercise a limited form of self government under provisions in the Indian Act. With funds provided by the federal government, supplemented in some cases with local rates, bands can provide such physical services within their communities as roads, water and sewage disposal; subject to criteria required by the senior governments with jurisdiction, bands may also operate schools and provide welfare services such as child protection and social allowances for the indigent. Also, band councils can manage reserve based lands and resources for use by band members, in band enterprises or for use by non-Indians to generate band revenue.

However, many Aboriginal leaders at band, regional and national level, now speak of sovereignty. They argue an inherent right to self-government with law-making powers far beyond local government provisions available at the discretion of Canada.

Also, the courts have confirmed the notion of unextinguished Aboriginal rights. In its 1990 judgment on the Sparrow case, the Supreme Court of Canada established that a member of the Musqueam Band in British Columbia had a constitutionally protected Aboriginal right to fish in the water at the mouth of the Fraser River, above and beyond the regulatory powers of the federal Department of Fisheries and Oceans.

Out of these concepts of sovereignty and Aboriginal rights grows the notion of hundreds of First Nations, with populations ranging from several score to a few thousand in some cases, scattered throughout the land mass of Canada, governing their lands and their people, and perhaps their people even off their lands, and managing resources such as fisheries outside their lands but within traditional territories, all separately from the provincial and federal jurisdictions surrounding them.

If today's "Aboriginal" people were fully Aboriginal, this concept, difficult though it might be in application, would carry with it a greater logic. But what will we make of the situation that many of the people with the Aboriginal right to fish at times and places to all other people in Canada are far more European Canadian than Aboriginal, both genetically and culturally?

In the Umbrella Final Agreement between the Government of Canada and the Council for Yukon Indians, you can be a beneficiary and entitled, for example, to hunt game animals such as moose, of either sex and at any time of the year, if you were 25% or more of Indian ancestry and ordinarily resident in the Yukon between 1800 and 1940 or are a descendant of such a person. As the descendant of such a person you no longer need the minimum 25% of Indian ancestry—you could be less than 1% of Indian ancestry, work in a government office in Whitehorse on a good annual salary in the bargain, and be free to hunt moose out of season.

(The Europeans arrived late in the Yukon, with the first major settlement consequent on the gold rush of 1898 to the Klondike district. The principal negotiators of the Yukon claim on the Aboriginal side were descendants of those who came in the gold rush or shortly thereafter. One beneficiary of the claim, a widely respected elder, tells how his father hiked over the pass in 1898 with the gold seekers to find his mother among the Indians of the Interior).

Let us suppose that these "nations" make their own laws in the area of family violence and child protection. Reading the Aboriginal Justice Inquiry, the Fatality Inquiries Act and the Child Advocacy Project reports out of Manitoba we see how successfully the male-dominated band leadership on reserves there has frustrated the protection of children from sexual abuse under Canadian law. What can we expect when these same leaders start making their own law?

Is it surprising when the Quebec Women's Association asks that the "(Canadian) Charter of Rights and Freedoms apply to Native governments"?

Can we understand when Sharon McIvor, speaking for the Native Women's Association of Canada, is reported to have expressed concern about the advent of native self-government and separate criminal justice systems?

Are we not increasingly doubtful that the solution to violence and sexual abuse will be found in Aboriginal self-government when we read news reports that the Naukana Native Women's Association on south Vancouver Island is "fighting for changes to the way reserve life is run so that it is better for women" and that a native women's conference in December, 1993 talked about "the need for native communities to heal themselves before they start governing themselves?"

Significantly, *Taking Our Rightful Place: Brief to the Royal Commission on Aboriginal Peoples*, Quebec Native Women's Association, 1993, stated:

> (It is) important to us to let you know how we feel about the Canadian Charter of Rights and Freedoms in relation to the eventual establishment of Native governments . . . We are convinced that the rights protected by virtue of the Canadian Charter of Rights and Freedoms are, on the whole, fundamental human rights as recognized by international law. . . . we ask that the Charter apply to Native governments for as long as there is no Native charter or charters giving us a higher or at least equal degree of protection.

In its recommendations, the Association asked the Commission to:

> . . . grant first priority to the family violence issue . . .

To the credit of the negotiators on both sides, the Yukon Umbrella Final Agreement provides that:

> Self-government agreements shall not affect the rights of Yukon Indian People as Canadian citizens

but goes on to raise anxiety when it then says:

> and unless otherwise provided pursuant to a self-government agreement or legislation enacted thereunder, their entitlement to all of the services, benefits and protections of other citizens applicable from time to time.

Does that tell us that a Yukon First Nation could, in fact, pass legislation under a self-government agreement that could effectively deprive its people of protections afforded other Canadian citizens?

I profoundly believe that women and children in Aboriginal communities, living anywhere in Canada, are and should always be entitled to all federal, provincial and territorial laws for the protection of human rights, Aboriginal rights notwithstanding. Entitled, indeed, to a far greater level of protection than is presently available to them as those laws are presently administered and enforced by Canada, the provinces and the territories.

The fundamental problem in Aboriginal communities in the nineteen-nineties, the root cause of the grief and the misery, is a devastating vulnerability to alcoholism which has resulted in heavy alcoholic drinking of the worst sort, with all its brutal consequences: violent assaults on women by their men, sexual abuse of women and children, gross neglect of children, solvent and gasoline sniffing by neglected and abused children while their parents drink, and a succession of violent deaths, increasingly by suicide among the neglected, sexually-abused, gasoline-sniffing youth.

An epidemic of AIDS, with the power to kill whole communities, is virtually inevitable.

Settling outstanding land claims and venturing into self-government, for which there is much to be said for other reasons, will be no solution to any of that.

I believe that only an urgent and direct attack on alcoholism among Aboriginal people will prevent the deaths of thousands of people. All the energy of every Aboriginal leader should be committed to this front, with major support from other responsible governments.

HOW A PEOPLE DIE

1

L aw enforcement in Davis Bay and in Kwatsi, the adjoining
Indian village, on a Friday night was an unpleasant business but it was hardly complicated.

All the single loggers in a twenty-mile radius converged on
the Golden Gate Hotel in the early evening to get drunk,
deliberately and efficiently, after the fashion of loggers. The
liquor lounge and the beer parlor alike boomed with the shouting and the hustling and large exhaust fans blew a stream of
sodden reeking air into the street.

Then at closing time, laden with cases of beer against the
drought that would prevail until opening Saturday morning, this
barbarous mob poured out in search of anything usable in the
way of a woman and a place to go on drinking.

The first dispersal used to be to the Silver Grill Cafe where
most women available could be found and dealt for, hostilities
engendered until fighting broke out and parties gathered
against the long hours before the dawn. But the damage exceeded the trade and after one riotous night in which three
tables and fourteen chairs had been mobilized as weapons and
reduced to bits and pieces, the old Chinese who garnered his
living by the place took to shutting it down before the mob hit
the street.

Now the immediate action formed on the sidewalk in front

of the hotel. There Corporal Thompson of the Davis Bay detachment of the Royal Canadian Mounted Police, lean and immaculate and quietly but doggedly persistent in the enforcement of the law, met it, cooled it and dispersed it as best he could. He then settled down with Constable Dyke, his no less able but deceptively chunky and slow-moving assistant, to the long hours of patrols by which they hoped to keep the later stages of revelry somewhere in the woodwork of parked cars, hotel rooms and a few private dwellings among the shacks along the foreshore.

And in the Indian village. Always a carload or more of loggers with booze would strike out for the Indian village to start up a party amid the clutter and filth of any of half a dozen houses in the village where entry could be had—and a good deal else— night or day so long as wine, beer or whisky cleared the passage.

Corporal Thompson had tried to stop that traffic. He and the Chief, old Billy Williams, had talked about it a lot after the people had first moved from the isolation of Hugger's Inlet to the new Indian Affairs houses on the Kwatsi Reserve a mile out of Davis Bay.

Billy had been anxious to stop it and unlike Corporal Thompson he had yet to give up trying. Without Billy's persistence the people might never have moved from their isolated home in the inlet, and with the same persistence he now tried to protect them from the complete dissolution he had always known would be the risk of moving to Davis Bay.

"It was for the kids, you know," Corporal Thompson had listened to him explain again and again. "We have to give the kids a better chance. The old people not gonna make it, you know. But we got to do it for the kids, so they got school and hospital. Some people gonna drink too much an' spoil it for themselves, you know. We can't help that, you know, but you got to stop those white guys bringin' drink in here, you know."

Corporal Thompson thought that he knew and he set at once to stopping the traffic. The next marauding white men found themselves before the magistrate promptly the following morning.

But it wasn't that easy. One of the accused men asked for a remand so he could hire a lawyer. When the case was heard a week later, justice had lost not only her swiftness but her sureness too.

The charge had been laid as a trespass under the Indian Act. But while the act specified that trespass on a reserve is an offense, it provided no definitions and with quiet glee the defending lawyer ridiculed the proposition that trespass could occur when one man agrees to have another in his house.

"Would my friend suggest that Indian people have any less right than other citizens to choose their associates? Perhaps that the law should pass on the suitability of their visitors?

And he called as a witness a resident of the village who said sure, he wanted these guys to visit him, any time they felt like it.

It became clear, painfully, to Corporal Thompson that neither he nor the Chief had any right to interfere unless the people whose homes the loggers and liquor went into had some objection to it.

But it was impossible for old Billy to see this. The manifest evil was so clear to him that the more Corporal Thompson tried to explain why they couldn't prevent it, the more certain the old man became that neither Thompson nor the magistrate cared a damn about what happened to his people. He was too polite to say it, but Thompson knew the difference between an old Indian coming full of trust for the protection of his people and the same old Indian when the hurt was in his eyes and he asked for help that wasn't there.

But he persisted. Indeed he did. He had a telephone installed in his house and when the cars came into the village late at night to spew their trouble, he'd phone Corporal Thompson.

"Them guys here again, Mr. Thompson. You gotta stop them guys, you know."

Thompson would patrol to the village but the pattern was soon established and everybody knew their parts by heart.

He'd knock on the door and when someone answered he'd ask: "Is everything all right here? Are these white guys bothering you?"

"Oh, everythin' all right, Mr. Cop. These guys, they friends of ours."

"You sure now?"

"Oh, we sure all right." Although half the time they wouldn't know the white men by name.

"O.K. Just thought I'd ask."

Then off to the Chief's house to explain that the people in the house didn't mind the white men being there.

"Course they don't mind. Them guys, they got a bunch of wine an' beer."

Thompson tried a different approach. He went to the village during the quieter days of the week and gathered together the Chief and some of the people whose houses were becoming regular weekend nightclubs. Then he went over the whole problem with them as sociably and informally as he could. He wore civilian dress instead of his uniform and sat down in their houses as though the stench and dirt didn't sicken him so much he couldn't eat a meal after he left.

He thought he made headway because everyone professed that they didn't really like the way things were going. They didn't really want to drink but these white guys pressed it on them. So he explained that he could help them stop it but that they would have to forbid the white men to come in and persist with the attempt to keep them out until the patrol arrived, then give evidence in court that they had done so.

"Well, that's pretty hard for us."

"But you'll have to try if I'm going to help."

"Well, we'll try."

But it did no good. The Chief kept phoning, the police kept patrolling and the people kept on saying these white guys, they our friends.

So finally Corporal Thompson went over the whole problem one last time with Billy then quit going out in response to the telephone calls. Sometimes the Chief would call three or four times but it was no use. He'd have gone on the instant if there had been any new or different ingredient in the complaint but there never was. The Chief was hurt and Thompson knew it and had agonies over it but he had hardened himself against what was happening in the village and the futility of his trying to alter it.

Which didn't help a damned bit when the night the baby died the Chief had phoned no less than four times.

2

I t was a quarter past nine Saturday morning when the call came about the baby. Dyke had just come back after four hours sleep to let Thompson away until midafternoon when they would break shift again in order to be together once more for the evening.

Thompson was about to leave when the telephone rang. He hesitated, looked at Dyke, shrugged his shoulders, sighed, then picked it up. "Might just see what this is." Then into the telephone: "RCMP Davis Bay detachment. Corporal Thompson speaking."

"That you, Thompson?"

"Yes, Billy."

"You got to come out here. I got Sammy Joseph in my house here right now. His baby die. His baby die some time in night time."

"Be right there, Billy. Meet you at Sammy's house. You stay with him till I get there."

"O.K."

Thompson hung up. "Baby died. Sammy Joseph's. During the night he says. That was Billy." And together they went out to the car.

The old Chief was waiting in front of the house when they drove up. His large body, set on disproportionately short legs, reflected the solidity which Thompson had come to recognize in him more than anything else. His village might turn to salt, it was hard to believe it wouldn't, but Billy Williams would still be ready to put it all on his back and carry it to safety if only the people would let him.

Billy led them into the house. Thompson took a deep breath before the door opened and held it until he was inside, then he let it out very slowly, steeling himself against the next breath he must take in. It was always the worst. When he finally had to take it he pressed his gloved fist against his nose to mix the smell of leather with the overwhelming stench of filth and squalor which saturated the atmosphere of the house. He'd never actually thrown up but neither did he ever feel sure he wouldn't. After another moment he let his hand down and began to take in his surroundings.

There'd been a party and some attempt to clean up the signs of it before his arrival. But one empty liquor bottle lay on its side at the end of a tattered couch and on a greasy table top several chipped china mugs displayed the mouth stains of cheap wine. As well as the cups the table supported a scramble of dirty dishes and half eaten food. In the midst of it a loaf of store bread lay open and from this a boy of perhaps ten passed slices to a younger girl and a much younger boy. This smallest child was naked save for a dirty undershirt. His legs and feet were black with grime. Thompson tried to sort between the humanity and the filth, to focus on something which would make a beginning.

The long room they had entered served as a kitchen and living room. From it, one door led into a bedroom on the left and centrally a short hallway led into a cubicle that might someday be a bathroom. A door on either side of the short hallway led to two more rooms. Thompson knew the floor plan. Probably fifteen out of the twenty-odd houses on the reserve were identical.

Sammy Joseph stood in the entrance to the hallway, his face immovably vacant. Thompson couldn't remember seeing him any other way.

"Where's the baby?"

Sammy might have heard, might not. The Chief motioned with his hand in the direction beyond Sammy and together he and Thompson went through to another room.

There was a crib in one corner with a dirty blanket over its contents; against one wall there was a bed. What remained of the floor space was used up with a tattered mattress and heaps of rags which might still be clothing.

Eliza Joseph, Sammy's wife, sat slouched on the bed, her hands at her face, a face distorted and drunken. The sickly sweet smell of liquor-heavy breath emerged even through the fetid air of the small room.

Thompson went to the crib and drew back the blanket. The lifeless body of a child less than a year lay on its back in fouled covers, the face fallen to one side, the nose draining mucus which, mixing with the dirt in the blanket, had formed a crust around the mouth.

Thompson covered the child and closed his eyes while he struggled to control the nausea and the sudden rage. He weathered the nausea but the rage began to smoulder deep down.

He began to shake and the vacant impassivity on Sammy's face triggered an urge to violence. He resisted grabbing the man, his training alone preventing it.

"Why didn't you go to the doctor?"

There was no reply, nothing. No response, no fright, no acknowledgement of Thompson's fury. Nothing.

Thompson all but screamed. "Why the hell didn't you go to the doctor?"

Then: "I told my wife she should take the kid to doctor. I told her. But I don't know why she don't take it. Maybe she don't know that kid is bad sick." Thompson turned away. Futility had displaced rage. Like bloody animals, he thought, and he was startled at how easily he let himself think it. Like bloody animals. No. Worse than animals. Animals don't leave their young to die in their own filth.

He turned to the Chief. "I want to use your phone." And they walked out, followed by Dyke who had never got beyond the front room where he'd been trying all that time not to breathe.

3

Dr. Cooper picked up the telephone, giving his head a shake at the same time. Saturday mornings weren't quite his mornings. It was almost ten but he never reckoned to be on top of a Saturday much before noon.

"Cooper here."

"This is Corporal Thompson. I'm out at the reserve. A baby died here during the night and I'd like you to take a look."

"Well, I'll see it anyway for the autopsy. Can't you just bring it in?"

There was a pause. Then: "I want you to see this one in her natural surroundings—if you can call it that."

The note in the voice conveyed urgency. It puzzled Dr. Cooper but urgencies were his business. He never asked for elaborations. "Be right there." And it wasn't any longer Saturday morning in which Dr. Cooper was never quite on top before noon. It was any working day and Dr. Cooper was on call. Nothing but his work would have his attention again until whatever the job he was finished with it.

Dr. Cooper regarded himself as an observant man and it was consistent with his attitude to his profession that he thought himself unexceptional in being so.

But he did comment to himself sometime later that it was odd he should have noticed more particularly than anything else in all that house the bucket on the floor amid the debris in the cubicle that must once have been intended to be a bathroom.

He took in a lot else during the short time in the house: the stench and the grime, the pervading dirt that covered the floor and rose up the walls, the clutter underfoot of old clothing turned to rags, the half-clothed children with running noses foraging bread out of the debris on the broken table, the chairs with their once glossy vinyl covers now shredded and the padding in tatters and as black with accumulated dirt as everything else.

But it was the bucket that he recalled most persistently afterward.

It was an enamel bucket of the kind sold as diaper pails and through the stains running down its outer sides you could see the bright white finish made in an invitation to cleanliness, such a bright white finish as a housewife might rinse and wipe and scald daily against the least chance of germs and odors and unsightliness.

But by its accumulated stains Dr. Cooper doubted this one ever had more than a swish in the sea, perhaps not even that.

It was full.

It was more than full. The urine and the solids together had reached the top and then, with children still using it in the night perhaps, it had begun spilling over the rim, the rolled white enamel rim, which had been made that way to be easy to clean.

As the contents had spilled over the edge, something substantial had come to lodge on the handle that rested against the side of the bucket.

And on the floor the stain of the spilling over crept outward and into the tattered rags of clothing which, though pushed aside to make a place for the bucket, hadn't been removed quite far enough.

Dr. Cooper remembered the bucket.

He also looked at the body of the child in the crib. A poorly fixed diaper had failed to contain her accumulated feces and she had died amid the fouled covers of her bed.

But he looked only briefly and then he turned to Thompson. "I can't do any more here. I can determine the rest in autopsy. You can have her brought in?"

"Right away. I just wanted you to see the condition she died in."

"For a particular reason?"

"I may charge these people with neglect."

"I see." Dr. Cooper glanced at the woman slouched on the bed who might be unaware of everything about her for all she showed. Then he looked at the man who stood just outside the little room, in the cubicle where the bucket was. "Is this your child?"

Impassively, the man nodded.

On his way out he stopped as the man shuffled aside to let him by.

"Why don't you empty that bucket?"

Nothing.

"I said, why don't you empty that bucket?"

Sammy Joseph looked a long time at him then in a listless monotone: "I tell the kids to pack that bucket out. I don't know why he don't pack it out. That's what I tell him, he should pack that out. Me, I go outside. I don't use that bucket."

4

T he trouble, Dr. Cooper thought, was that the simple maxims of survival no longer apply.

Before all the paraphernalia of the modern society—medical science with its phalanx of technology and equipment and doctors and nurses, social welfare agencies to parcel out subsistence and apprehend the victims of neglect, preventive immunology to limit the ravage of disease, government housing to house those who would never have housed themselves—before all that the children of the ineffectual parents survived in such few numbers.

In an animal species living directly in the natural environment, those faulty by the standards of the species will fail to survive long enough to reproduce in any quantity. In the same way it had always come about that the slovenly people, unable to function effectively in the social and economic environment of man's less advanced communities, would bring only a few of their children to survive into adulthood.

But now society steps into the breach, not far enough to protect the child from the squalid wasteland of incompetence, but far enough to keep him alive to grow up in it, to suffer by it and in turn to reproduce his own children into it.

In the best of good conscience we have said that there shall be life for everyone.

But the reproductive capacity of man, like that of all beings, is not a matter of good conscience: it is an ingredient in the survival of our species. The reproductive capacity strives to fill a void. To ensure survival of the race it has a power to repopulate rapidly following on disaster or to fill with burgeoning suddenness any new space created by discovery or technology.

But when the habitat is full there is competition for survival and the race is served by the success and reproduction of the fit, the weeding out of the weak, the disabled and the ineffective.

The dynamics of this process are not kind. They serve the race, not the individual. Nature tolerates with equanimity the perishing of some and the surviving of others.

But now modern man has decided to defy nature. He has said that everyone to whom life has been given by the persistent capacity of man to reproduce shall have the use of some space, the opportunity to live, the opportunity in turn to reproduce.

The strong shall care for the weak, the few shall provide for the many, the fortunate shall succor the unfortunate, society shall mother and ensure life for all her children.

Not only the fit survive. So also do the unfit.

It is so very decent. Dr. Cooper, whose knowledge and skills were devoted to restoring and preserving life began to wonder if, ultimately, it was workable.

5

C orporal Thompson had fifteen years in the force, serving in rural and small municipal detachments in British Columbia where local Indian populations reeled in their struggle with alcohol.

It had been prior to his service that Indians could in no way legally possess or consume alcoholic drinks of any sort. He had lived then in Williams Lake where his father had finished his service and retired from the now disbanded BC police.

There were few detachments outside Williams Lake through the whole of the Cariboo in those days and indeed no need of any. The hinterlands of that cow town were sparsely populated by ranchers preoccupied with working their lands and cattle and surviving the depression. Here and there far apart were Indian reserves of a wide range of sizes and settlements.

Most Indian families had some horses and a few head of beef cattle and rights to a piece of meadow on the reserve where they cut hay to feed their stock in the winter.

A few had substantial herds, good small ranching operations by any standards. Those who had very little of their own worked out for the white ranchers in the haying season and did a little trapping in the winter.

Everybody was poor, white or Indian. Even the large ranches looked in ruins with beef at five cents a pound on the hoof. The man who contracted hay at a dollar a ton in the stack or joined the ranch crew at a dollar a day and his board often had more to show for it after the steers were sold in the fall than the rancher himself.

With everybody on their uppers it didn't occur to anyone, white or Indian, that the Indians were underprivileged or that they suffered under a suffocating paternalism.

There no doubt was paternalism, depending on what you meant by the word. Thompson had travelled, when he wasn't in school, out into the back country with his father on patrol. They stopped at Indian villages that were accessible by road and there was a considerable display of respect on both sides. The Indians all knew his father, they called him Mishter Dompshon in the molasses slow drawl of their labored English, he called them by Chowloo or Pete or Billy—whatever first name they used, Indian or English.

They seemed childishly happy to see him and there was much smiling and nodding along with labored talk—except when his father put specific questions about some misdemeanor in which case there would still be much smiling but no more talking or nodding.

A few times he and his father made joint patrols with the Indian agent. Corporal Thompson's recollections from these trips were of a powerfully decisive but kindly man who listened to plaints of poverty, marital disputes or problems about irrigation ditches, all with equal patience, then gave out clothing, rendered judgements or ordered work to be done as a patriarch might in his own family. The boy gained the impression that the people did do as he told them and that they were satisfied of the wisdom of his instructions but of course it may have been only an impression.

It was paternalism all right, Thompson reflected, and that's pretty bad stuff according to the papers nowadays and the reason the Indians are in such a bad way. Yes, sir. All that stifling paternalism. No chance to live their own lives. Under the thumb of the government all the time. Never learned to make a decision on their own. Well, maybe. But it was damn remarkable how the

Indian agent in Williams Lake must have kept all the Indians from living their own lives or making their own decisions when he had such a large territory to cover that he reached some of the more remote reserves less than once a year. Now wait a minute, Thompson. You're getting worked up again about all this unrealism about Indians nowadays. Yeh. Okay. Simmer down.

There was a little trouble in town of course. Indians liked to come into Williams Lake and whoop it up a bit and there was a fluctuating business in back alleys and livery barns, especially at stampede time, in wine and rotgut whisky.

Sometimes even out on the reserves there'd be a little excitement following a home brew party but nothing that ever amounted to much. It all made very little work now and again for the police.

But after the war there was a prosperity such as hardly any Indians and few white men had seen before and a fair sprinkling of Indian men came back from a time of military service and equality. The pressure began to build for granting equal liquor privileges to Indians.

Old Thompson retired about that time but his concern for Indian people stayed very much alive. He understood the arguments for putting everyone on the same footing but he thought he knew his Indians well enough to predict disaster. It was going to be damned expensive equality and the Indians were going to pay the price.

In the event, a compromise was granted in which Indians could drink by the glass in the beer parlors but couldn't buy anything from the parlors or the government liquor stores to take home.

The disaster materialized. The Indians converged on the one place where lawfully they could drink, the beer parlors, and all hell was to pay. Since most of the beer parlors in the Cariboo were located in Williams Lake, most of the paying was done right within the confines of that hitherto fair to middling peaceful place on the frontier.

Some used the phrase "piled up like cordwood" to describe the accumulation of passed-out Indians which developed after closing time in the vicinity of the parlors—the rather predictable consequence of a now you can, now you can't regulation of drinking. Since you couldn't carry any away in a carton, you tried to carry it all away in your stomach.

Piled up like cordwood. The phrase stuck in the younger Thompson's memory. It epitomized the change in attitude of the townspeople to disgust and revulsion, sometimes, at best, of a you-can't-blame-them-it's-our-fault-not-theirs kind of looking down, but even in that there was contempt.

But a change from what? It was hard for Thompson to remember. He knew his father's attitude, he thought, and he remembered bitter words between his father and others following on some phrase that granted less than humanity to Indian people. "Some of that smoked meat," he remembered once in reference to an Indian woman and there'd damned nearly been blows.

Still there hadn't been, he thought, the disgust and revulsion before the terrible spectacle created by opening the beer parlors to them. There had been respect and courtesy in the stores and the hospital and in the government offices. But was that really the town? Did the town really have an attitude? Perhaps the town just ignored the Indian people, apart from necessary trade which, after all, was as profitable to the town as to the Indians.

Thompson, in his memory, was not sure. Because really, apart from the visits on patrol with his father and the evident relationship that existed between his father and many Indian people, his abundant impressions began after the beer drinking started.

In a few short years, good men were reduced to alcoholism and poverty. The cattle were sold, the hay mowers rusted in the long grass of the uncut meadows, and the horses pawed the snow for last summer's grass to see them through the winter.

Men fought with their wives, families broke up, children were neglected and a death toll from accidents and violence in which alcohol was inevitably the decisive factor filled the pages of the small town papers.

The optimistic said, well, it's going to take time, isn't it? I mean, you can't expect *this* generation to adjust to it. But we had to make a start sometime, didn't we? When the next lot grows up, they'll be used to the privilege and they'll take it in their stride.

Others said, damn it, why this stupid halfway business? Can't anyone *realize* that it's this business of not being able to take it out that makes it so bad? What would *you* do if you could only drink in the parlors and you knew that, bang, at eleven o'clock you're cut off till ten o'clock tomorrow morning? You'd do the same thing they're doing and so would I. Knock back glass after glass right up to the wire then stagger out on the street and pass out. For God's sake, give them the whole thing.

A few said, damn it, I told you this would happen but everybody had the equality kick and now look what we've done. We've made beggars and paupers and tramps of the lot of them, standing around with their tongues hanging out, waiting for the parlors to open in the morning.

The senior Thompson, retired now, didn't say much at all. But his son, finishing high school and already with an application made to enlist in the RCMP, sensed the old man's sadness. Once after a comment had been made to him, which formerly he would have leaped upon, the old man turned away and tears came to his eyes. It had become too much, the sight of men who had once had dignity and a family gathered around them, a little meadow they hayed and a few head of cattle, the respect of the neighboring ranchers as well as their own tribesmen, all now reduced to grovelling for change to buy beer.

It was RCMP policy not to post a man back to his home ground but for Thompson an exception was made because of a lingering illness which kept his mother in pain for ten years before her death. He was rotated on a number of postings throughout British Columbia. He began in the mid north, and then served through the south and east. He knew Terrace and Hazelton on the Skeena River, then Smithers, Burns Lake and Prince George. After that came the Okanagan with two years at each of Kamloops, Armstrong and Penticton. Then he served in Cranbrook, followed by Creston and after that he came out to Davis Bay on the coast.

Police work wasn't the congenial, friend-of-the-citizen sort of pursuit it had been for his father and the realization at first profoundly disappointed him, especially in the relationship with Indian people. He was the cop, suspect at best, openly hated at worst. They were the drunks, in and out of the jails and the police courts in an endless round, eternally followed by sheets of blue paper, living, it seemed, constantly as described by Section 94(b) of the Indian Act, intoxicated off a reserve.

He worked it out in one posting: 87 per cent of the total cost of law enforcement for the detachment was devoted to that one section of the Indian Act—arresting, detaining, processing before the courts, escorting to jail. And his calculation did not take into account the cost of transport by aircraft to Oakalla Prison Farm of the people on longer sentences for repeated offenses.

A resigned and rather cheerful Indian prisoner once suggested to him during an escort duty that the Indians might as well buy the aircraft. So many of them flew to Vancouver so often to serve time in Oakalla, it would save the government money.

And if he suffered distress at the relationship with Indians his job imposed on him, it was surely compounded by the attitudes that developed around him in some of his colleagues. Perhaps without having known the people at least a little in the dignity of their own surroundings, they had nothing but the eternal round of arrests and court appearances to judge by. Some said openly that the only sober Indian was the one in jail the morning after. It was perhaps impossible not to feel profound dislike, even disgust. It was, after all, an unpleasant chore to deal constantly in a process which at best is hostile and underscored by force with a people whose standards of cleanliness more often than not were vastly different from one's own and who reeked of drink and frequently vomit besides.

But if it was unpleasant business for the police, what in hell must it be like for the Indians? And Thompson found himself flashing in anger at the callousness of the less thoughtful around him.

He argued with some vigor that they had better all damn well remember that the unfortunate Indians who couldn't cope with alcohol took up so much of their time—after all, it was the nature of the work—that they just didn't meet the men and women who stayed at their jobs and their homes and looked after themselves and their families.

He followed up on that idea once and in the end rather wished he hadn't.

He went into the local Indian Agency and reviewed the band lists with the superintendent. The object was to verify the number of Indian people who were not caught in the alcohol trap.

It was shattering. It was true that in almost every community there were a few who had command of their own lives; in the district there were several exceptional people, exceptional by any standards.

But the great majority over sixteen or seventeen years were in serious trouble with alcohol, most in an apparently hopeless stage, beyond recovery. In one reserve there was not one person who was not reasonably believed to drink to a problem level.

And the estimate was made by two men, a police officer and an Indian Affairs officer, who, whatever public stereotype they might suffer from, were committed to believe as well as they could of the people for whom they shared a responsibility. At least to the best of Thompson's conscience that was the case.

In time, the anomalous business of serving in the parlors only was given up in favor of identical rights for everyone. But this produced no startling results. Perhaps there was a shift to wine from beer and certainly drinking at home was a lot less expensive at liquor store rather than bootleg prices.

Then eventually the province instructed the force to abandon the practice of arresting and charging when the only offense was that of being drunk in a public place. This put an end to the treadmill though occasionally a drunk might be held overnight for his own safety then released in the morning. This new policy applied to both Indians and others, though it was doubtless to the Indians that it made most difference.

And to the police, Thompson thought, who could give up what may one day be seen in retrospect as the most futile sustained effort in law enforcement on a non-criminal issue in the history of Canada.

6

T hompson acted quickly following the death of Annette Joseph. The possibility that he would charge her parents remained only a possibility but it bore on what now took place.

The body was taken to the morgue and within hours a coroner's jury was convened and sworn. The jury viewed the body and Billy Williams answered the obvious questions put to him for its identification. The inquest was then adjourned to be convened again on receipt of a pathologist's report—unless, in the result, other lawful process overtook the uneventful deliberations of a coroner's jury. The body went out by the afternoon flight to Vancouver for autopsy. In a routine unattended death Dr. Cooper, multiple functionary—coroner, physician, pathologist—in the isolation of Davis Bay, would have done the autopsy but when charges might be laid on the results both Thompson and he agreed that it was prudent to distribute the responsibility into more hands.

The body was returned by Tuesday and could now be released to the family for burial. Thompson drove to the village himself to tell Billy that if he would see what the Joseph's wishes were about the body, the police would deliver it. Some families used the services of the undertaker in town, others tended their dead in their own traditions.

Billy said he would find out and let Thompson know.

With that accomplished there was little else to do. On the Saturday Dyke had taken statements from everybody they could determine had been in the house and from Billy since he had been the first informed by Sammy that the child had been found dead in the crib.

Thompson had been over the statements and found nothing more he'd have wanted to ask than Dyke had already pursued. Yes, the baby'd been sickly but no, nobody thought the baby was that bad they needed to take her to the doctor. Well, yes, they had been drinking a little all right. Maybe Eliza hadn't looked at the baby during the night but the baby hadn't been crying. About the diapers and the mess all over the crib? Well, the baby must have been changed the night before and if the baby didn't fuss nobody would wake her up just to change the diaper. At least that's what Winnifred thought. Anyway, it was the old lady's baby, not her baby, and anyway Sarah was there and she was the one should help the old lady with the kids cause Winnifred got three of her own.

When the old lady finally got the wine out of her system enough to talk she couldn't give anything but the vaguest replies to any questions. Dyke said it was like looking for a lost boat in a dense fog to try to penetrate the glassy stare and focus on something with her.

She didn't know when they'd started drinking. When had she changed her baby? Almost inaudibly, she didn't know. Well, had she changed her before supper or after supper? No response. Last night, maybe before dark? After it got dark? A slight nodding of the head. Which was it, before or after it got dark out? No response.

Sammy's answers were framed around a professed puzzlement as to why somebody else didn't do something. "Yeh, I tell her she should clean that kid up. I don't know why she don't clean that kid up."

As to where the booze came from or how much of it they drank, everybody was vague with the studied vagueness of evasion.

Scrupulously, Dyke had warned each of them that they didn't have to give a statement and that anything they did say might be used against them. It was routine whenever there was a clear question of responsibility for a death; it was more than routine in Dyke's mind when Thompson's anger flashed up over something the way it had over this.

So really there was nothing more to ask and certainly nothing more to ask old Billy, but Thompson stood awhile with him foraging for something to say that wouldn't just be an inanity and might restore a little of the warmth that once had been between them. Ever since Thompson had stopped coming out in response to Billy's phone calls about the cars coming into the village at night, Thompson had felt the change. A shutter had come down. It was nothing said, and it was imprecise, but it was in the looking away when Thompson spoke. And there was no escape from it or way around it, only the certainty that the more one tried to heal it, the worse it became.

Finally: "They must have been drinking for quite a few hours. Any idea when they started?"

In a long silence Billy looked out over the sea in the direction of the distant mountains and the isolated inlet where the people once had lived. "When them guys came I guess."

"What guys?"

"Them white guys."

"Nobody mentioned any white men."

Billy brought his eyes slowly back from the distance to rest squarely on Thompson. Again for a long moment he said nothing and Thompson willed himself not to avert his own eyes from the penetration of the other.

Then: "I phoned you. I phoned you when they first come and I phoned you again after."

"But I didn't know it was Sammy's."

And then he said nothing, for what difference could it have made had he known. Neither had he known a child lay dying and he would not have come on this futile errand about white men and liquor.

Now he looked away under the pressure of the accusation and for a little while longer he endured the silence of this terrible misunderstanding that he had the power to make a law to fit the situation and then enforce it. The evil was so manifest; it only confirmed the meanness of the police that rather than attack it, they made complicated and obscure excuses that it wasn't their business.

Faced by the certainty of this conviction in the old man's mind, Thompson made a feeble apology and left.

7

T hompson asked Dyke to go back and tell the people who'd been in that house that he knew there'd been white men there during the night the baby died and he wanted their names.

"Right now?"

Thompson considered that, knowing of course the point of the question. Then: "All right. Wait till the child is buried. It probably won't be that much use anyway. In the meantime I'll see Cooper."

Dr. Cooper held clinic in the afternoons and had morning rounds at the hospital. He could see Thompson between eleven-thirty and twelve-thirty the next morning and he would come to the detachment. He'd appreciate the change from his own surroundings.

They met, therefore, in Thompson's office.

Thompson told him in a few words the contents of the report from Vancouver. "Pneumonia. Substantial infection in a rash and sores on the buttocks and thighs."

Cooper nodded.

Then: "Plain English, what did Annette Joseph, aged eleven months, fourteen days and some hours die from, Jack Cooper?"

Dr. Cooper had a face that with a barely perceptible shift could convey much the same as a shrug of the shoulders. He shrugged. "Just what the report says."

"The report is the usual acme of clinical detachment. The report was not Annette's doctor in her short life. The report has never known the Sammy Josephs. The report did not visit the Kwatsi Reserve last Saturday morning."

"The child was never strong, you know."

"Why?"

Dr. Cooper's face let go the shrug and took on a thoughtful-ness, a rather intent thoughtfulness. "Why do you ask?"

"I want to know what killed the child. What really killed the child."

"Yes, I realize that. I meant why do you ask in this particular case? Killed is a pretty strong word."

"Because I think someone might very reasonably be held accountable—before the courts."

"I see." The shrug look again. "Chronic malnutrition for one. The child has never been properly fed. Also a great deal of localized skin infection. Diaper rash getting infected and spreading down the legs."

"I didn't notice that when I looked in the crib."

"You wouldn't. Not until you scrape off the crust of dried pus and dirt. But it was bad. Particularly bad I should say. I don't shock easily but it turned me a bit I must admit. I'm rather glad I didn't do the autopsy."

Thompson sought about for his next question. Then: "Would ordinary care have kept the child alive?"

"What is ordinary care?"

The counter question came so quickly it surprised Thompson.

"Just...ordinary care. Damn it, don't be obtuse. Ordinary care is feeding a kid and keeping it clean and taking it to the doctor when it's sick."

"Perhaps. But by whose standards?" Then without waiting for an answer: "I can tell you that if Sammy and his wife had fed the kid a little better and kept her clothing and bedding clean and brought her to the clinic when she got sick, not after she was in a crisis, she'd have lived."

"They didn't take her at all."

"But they did earlier on, you know. They had the youngster in several times before. In fact she was probably in the hospital as much as at home."

"You gave Sammy's wife instructions about feeding?"

"Oh sure. But you're talking to the wall."

"But the fact remains, if she'd been paying attention to the kid, she would have known she needed to go for medical help."

"Yes, I guess you could say that." But Dr. Cooper spoke with a sigh, as though he couldn't deny the argument Thompson put forward, but couldn't accept it either.

"Well, what's wrong with that? What's wrong with the simple proposition that if parents neglect a child and it dies when it needn't, they can damn well be held responsible?"

The shrug look again and this time it began to annoy

Thompson. But then Dr. Cooper rose to his feet and stared a long time out the window and Thompson waited in a certainty that there was more to come.

Finally: "I think it is easy to fix responsibility, very difficult to fix culpability. I do not think that Sammy and his wife chose to belong to an outcast people. I do not think they chose to be fundamentally confused by the world about them. I do not think it was their idea that they have such a susceptibility to alcohol they are utterly useless in its presence. I do not think—and maybe this is the only important point—that they chose to live by the standards they were born into but be judged by the standards others have decided to apply to them.

"I know this particular death is pretty horrible to think about—the sores and the dirt and all that—but it really isn't fundamentally different from ten or twelve others over the past five or six years.

"Perhaps the real problem is not the ones who die but the ones who live. We keep the majority of them alive in spite of how their parents live, and they grow up geared to do the same thing all over again to their next generation."

Something in the detachment of Dr. Cooper's almost whimsical analysis of life and death, the quietly spoken words which verged on being idly spoken words, tripped again the flash of anger that had beset Corporal Thompson beside the crib and the dead infant on Saturday morning.

He hit the desk and got up from his chair in one movement. Dr. Cooper turned in mild surprise. Thompson looked him evenly in the eyes then found his words: "I see it another way. I see it like it is one goddamn crying shame for a kid to die in a stinking foul crib in her own dirt, half starved and ignored while her parents can't think of anything but where the next drink is coming from. The hell with your different standards. I don't *care* who's an Indian and who's a white man. I care what it must have been like to be Annette Joseph for eleven miserable months and die without the chance to live."

"Do you intend to lay charges?"

"Yes."

"I'll help you all I can. I only wish I could believe it would do any good."

As soon as Dr. Cooper left, Corporal Thompson slipped the long blue form into the typewriter and began hammering the keys:

> This is the information of Corporal James Acheson Thompson on behalf of Her Majesty The Queen. The informant says that he has reasonable and probable grounds to believe and does believe that Sammy Joseph and Elizabeth Joseph on or about Friday, July 25, 1969 A.D. at Kwatsi village near Davis Bay in the County of Prince Rupert and Province of British Columbia did unlawfully expose Annette Joseph a child under the age of ten years and did thereby endanger her life CONTRARY TO THE FORM OF STATUTE THEREIN MADE AND PROVIDED.

When he was done he telephoned Magistrate Earl. Within the hour he had sworn it out. There was no going back.

8

L ater in the day he talked to Dyke again. Dyke had run into a wall trying to learn anything about the white men. The Chief could tell him nothing about their car and the Joseph family wouldn't tell him anything except that there were two of them, they didn't know their names, they hadn't asked them to come, they didn't know why they were there and one by one they disclaimed having had anything to do with them.

"I don't know why them guys comin' in here. I tell them girls, they shouldn't let them white guys comin' in here all the time."

Thompson reflected on the meagreness of this information, considering the course to which he had committed himself earlier. Then to Dyke: "I've laid a charge, you know. Criminal Code, Section 189. Against both Sammy and Elizabeth."

"Thought you probably would. You had the look in your eye. It's going to be a hard one to make stick."

Thompson had never doubted that. It was the tough ones to

make stick that he usually felt strongest about in the sense of grievance that often brought him into court on behalf of the Crown.

"What do we know so far?"

Dyke opened a folder in which he had collected the statements he had taken and the facts he had observed. Thompson waited while he leafed about in these papers and the leafing about, Thompson knew, was time buying. For in his mind Dyke was sorting the question, what do we know, and the sorting was not favorable to the task Thompson's charge had set upon them.

Then Dyke began and the summary was rapid and complete, treating the obvious impartially with the obscure, and couched at times in the phraseology that would ultimately be used in an official report. "The Joseph family lives in a one-story frame house of recent construction on the Kwatsi Reserve, a little less than a mile from Davis Bay.

"The Kwatsi village consists of some twenty-two houses of very similar construction and is occupied by Indian people of the Kwatsi band who moved there from an isolated location in Hugger's Inlet four years ago.

"The Joseph house has a front room which serves as a kitchen and living area. Leading off from it are one bedroom and a hallway to a cubicle which might have been intended to be a bathroom. This hallway gives access to two other small bedrooms.

"The family consists of Sammy Joseph, forty-seven, his wife Elizabeth (known as Eliza), forty-two, Sarah, fifteen, Tommy, thirteen, Isaac, ten, Norma, seven, and Sam Junior, four. Annette was eleven months.

"There is another older daughter in the house. She is Winnifred, twenty-three years, and she has three children of her own: Nola, eight, Terry, three, and Marten, two months.

"Altogether there were twelve people living in the house as of Friday, July 25.

"The dwelling is sparsely furnished and crowded. It has electricity and running water to a cold tap in the sink. There is no indoor toilet facility.

"According to statements taken, all members of the family were at home on Friday, July 25. No one acknowledges that the baby, Annette, was seriously ill in the late afternoon or evening, or was restless and crying. They say she had a cold but several of the small children have had colds for quite a while. They always seem to have colds.

"Annette was given a bottle about eight in the evening but didn't seem to want it. Winnifred prepared the bottle and took it in to her. Elizabeth stood by the crib awhile trying to get her to take it. Nobody thought it unusual that she didn't take her bottle. She was left in her crib asleep at that time and no further notice was taken of her until she was discovered dead the next morning at nine.

"The statements are quite candid about the drinking. They are to the effect that Sammy brought home a gallon of wine late in the afternoon, between three-thirty and four-thirty, and the adults began drinking it. This is acknowledged to be Sammy, Eliza and Winnifred but no doubt includes Sarah and Tommy when the older people got drunk enough not to notice. But we'd never prove it. Around seven o'clock Jimmy Joseph, Sammy's brother, came in and drank some of the wine, then left. Two cupfuls as nearly as anyone remembers.

By eleven o'clock the wine was finished and the family were about to go to bed. Two white men arrived shortly after eleven and they brought some beer and whisky and some more wine. Nobody claims to know how much and nobody admits to knowing who they were or why they came or when they left.

"Everybody began drinking again and the next solid piece of information is that at nine the next morning Winnifred checked the baby and knew something was wrong. She called her father, who went to the Chief's house right away. The Chief says he could tell it was too late to do anything for the baby, so he called us instead of the doctor.

"I'm pretty sure about this business of the minor children drinking. It happens all the time at Kwatsi. We've found little ones intoxicated there and Sammy's no stricter than anyone else. But we don't *know* that Sarah and Tommy got into the booze."

Dyke looked up squarely at Thompson. "And that's all we know outside of Dr. Cooper's medical evidence and the autopsy report. Put it all together, it isn't very much."

"No. But my argument isn't very complicated either. All I'm saying is that with normal attention to the child they'd have known she was seriously ill and they'd have got help. If it had been too late, at least they would have tried. I'm relying on Jack Cooper's statement that the kid's illness would have been evident and that all that damn dirt and infection contributed to it. If that isn't neglect, what is? And I'm up to here with this argument that because they're Indians you have to make allowances. Kids are entitled to be cared for by their parents, and if we're going to tolerate less care for Indian kids because we think they have different standards to start with, then we're discriminating."

"You don't have to convince me. But you're going to have to convince the court and that might not be easy."

"Yes. I kind of think you're right. Damn it."

9

Sammy and Eliza came before Magistrate Earl to hear the charge and elect trial and Billy came with them to interpret. Thompson was not sure whether they fell back into their own language as they would a fortress for defense or whether in fact their English, sufficient perhaps to parry the intrusion of white men into the narrow arena of their lives, simply could not deal with the abstractions of the judicial process.

Billy interpreted the charge while they took the impassive stance of those to whom all is fate and the making of choice is so alien as to be wholly beyond comprehension. Thompson wondered how the words of the Criminal Code came out in the tribal tongue of the Northwest coast. Billy talked a long time in that strange language; when he had finished and said to the court—"they know what that charge mean now"—Thompson and Magistrate Earl found themselves utterly in Billy's debt for any assurance they ever would have that this due process was, in fact, one of justice.

"Now, Billy, explain to them that this is not the trial. Now they have to make a choice. They make a choice now about how they want to be tried. They can be tried by this court, that is to say if they want I can try them myself. Or they can be tried by a court comprised of a judge without a jury or they can be tried by a court comprised of a judge *and* a jury. I'll explain each of those choices carefully now and you interpret it to them."

The labor of speech went on, the labor of words and the labor of meaning, the deliberate and slowly spoken phrases of the court and the long intervals of the incomprehensible language spoken these days by fewer than a thousand souls.

Sammy and Eliza did not move. They did not answer in their eyes, nor in their face, nor in their hands; they only stood. And when it was all done Billy had in some way got from them a few nods and a word or two and all it meant was that they did not know which to choose, if indeed they understood they had a choice at all.

Magistrate Earl started again and this time he made clear that he would not wish to try them himself for fear that their difficulty in making a choice should be the reason for their ending up in his court.

Thompson stared into the papers on the table before him as though his concentration therein would shut out the ordeal of words. But he did not see the papers, he only went on hearing the words and the words struggled with meanings surely made obscure in the labor of translation and the mysteries of due process.

It somehow came to pass that they chose to be tried by a judge without a jury and it remained then to explain that a preliminary hearing would be held in Magistrate Earl's court to determine if, in fact, the evidence warranted their being put over for trial.

Understanding now became further impeded because though Billy himself had understood the earlier questions it took him a long time to fathom the difference between a preliminary hearing and a trial and why, if Sammy and Eliza had had the right to choose not to be tried by Magistrate Earl, Magistrate Earl now had the right to decide whether they would be tried at all.

Thompson did not believe anyone could have done a better

job of explaining; still, when Billy finally turned to Sammy and Eliza he could not believe either that understanding would be achieved. He felt suffocated by the confusion that lay behind the impassive faces and he longed to impose the clarity of his own distinctions and understanding.

But he knew he could do no better than Magistrate Earl and he waited now to take some step that would place on other shoulders the responsibility for making Sammy and Eliza understand, since he could do nothing himself to accomplish it.

The opportunity came when he had to speak about the date for the preliminary trial. He asked for two full weeks to assure that Sammy and Eliza could get legal aid.

"Corporal, do you think they're going to manage that?"

"I'll see to it."

"And in the interval?"

"The crown has no objection to their being released on their own recognizance."

Which was the end of the legal process for the time being.

10

T hompson had a case to make and he got on with it. The day after the court appearance he drove the thirty-five miles of winding road along the coast line to Yucla where the Indian Agency headquarters lay. He wanted to interview Arne Saunders, the Agency superintendent, who had charge of a number of Indian bands in the area and had been responsible for the move of the people now at Kwatsi from their old home in the isolation of Hugger's Inlet, seventy miles across the open strait.

Saunders was in and occupying his desk as though he had never quite come in from the outside; large hands handled papers as though they would have been happier swinging an axe, and a young, yet weathered face looked up from the gathered shoulders of a workingman's frame.

Thompson explained that he had come for some background on Sammy Joseph. Nothing much really, just whether he had been receiving assistance of any nature in the month or two preceding the child's death.

Saunders drew a file and confirmed it. "Yes. Steady assistance for months, years, I guess. Sammy, his wife and six children and an older daughter and her three children."

"He ever work?"

"He worked when he was in Hugger's Inlet. Not since."

"Wouldn't they be better off if he did work? No reason why he can't, is there?"

"Well, that's how I see it. But it's not how Sammy sees it."

"Can't you just cut him off? Force him to it?"

"It's a long story."

Thompson mulled in the silence Saunders gave him, then: "Yes, I guess it is. No need to go into it. I think I've a pretty fair idea. Anyway, the point for my purposes is that Sammy had the means of providing food and essentials to his children."

"You can say that. We've been issuing the rental allowance as well, even though he pays no rent on a subsidy house. Trying to be sure there's enough so the kids don't have to go without."

"From what I saw in the house, or didn't see, the kids are going without anyway. Do you issue it in cash?"

"Not any longer. We used to but it was pretty evident it wasn't reaching the kids. Bad alcohol problem. So now it goes to the store and they can draw it out in groceries and clothing. I still suspect they trade some of it off for booze but there's a limit to how much supervising you can do."

"You know about the baby?"

"Well, just that she died. Was there anything particular about it?"

"I've laid a charge against Sammy and his wife. Section 189 Criminal Code. Exposing a child."

Saunders was puzzled. "Exposing? You mean they left—"

"Matter of definition. The child died in her crib. The section says abandon or expose so that life is likely to be endangered. In the interpretation section abandon or expose includes dealing with a child in a manner that is likely to leave that child exposed to risk without protection. I'm arguing that by failing to get medical help and pay reasonable attention to the child so that they would have known she needed medical help, they dealt with her in a manner which exposed her to risk."

"I see." Saunders mulled in the silence now.

"You have doubts?" Thompson queried.

The other looked up quizzically. "Doubts? Doubts are my stock in trade. No, I just wonder about the usefulness of enforcement. Or anything else for that matter. Tell me what happened, exactly."

Thompson went over it for him and to both of them it sounded frighteningly ordinary. They agreed on that in the small shuddering comments of men whose routine is made up of the tragedy of others. "You think it'll stick?"

"It sounded likely at the time. Or appropriate. I'll confess I'm not so sure now. You think about Sammy and what kind of a start he must have had to be like he is and you think what he *is* like and you wonder if he can be held responsible for anything.

"But that's all I'm saying. That a man *is* responsible for looking after his baby. The immediate reason that child died is that Sammy and Elizabeth were so preoccupied with their own wants that they dealt with the child in a careless and offhand way. I don't know how else to describe it. And that's an offense."

Without words but in slow, rhythmic nods Saunders gave his assent to the argument, and Thompson rose, thanked him, then took his leave. Saunders rose to see him out, and once again Thompson found himself struck by the anomaly of that particular man being confined in the interior of a government office. It was a groundless notion if you thought about it, but there it was, and he wondered how Saunders had got into Indian Affairs.

11

A rne Saunders himself sometimes puzzled on the wholly unlikely fact that he was an employee of Indian Affairs.
The son of a self-made rancher, he'd been born in the

backwoods of British Columbia during the depression and raised into hard, unremitting labor and a profound distrust of the welfare state.

His father used to say he'd started the outfit on a sack of beans and a cow and chewed it out of the bush with his teeth. It was a small outfit, running a hundred head of part-bred Herefords in its best year, and it shared a valley with half a dozen other small outfits. Nobody made enough money until the war years to pay income tax and most men worked off their land tax by putting themselves and their teams and wagons onto the provincial road crew during the late spring and early summer, before the haying.

His father and mother, then Arne and each of his three brothers and two sisters as they grew up, labored long days in the round of wresting a living out of the hay meadows and the pine grass, the log fences and the irrigation ditches, the scrubby horses and the half-bred cattle. They labored and were thankful for the little their labor gained them. In 1947 they planned to buy a pick-up truck, the first motor vehicle they had ever seriously considered, but had to defer it another two years to use the money to send Arne and his younger brother out to high school. They counted it a blessing the boys had a chance to go to high school.

Men in the valley took their politics seriously, cussing out the government for land taxes, bad roads and for not working hard. The first two grievances rested on the only tangible points of contact they had with government, the last on the observation that politicians who had time to stump the country at elections couldn't be putting in the kind of day on the job their own experience taught them was at least necessary if not virtuous.

But apart from this, the valley was without government or at any rate the consciousness of government. Nobody thought the government owed them anything except roads, some schooling for their children through local boards and privacy. Certainly the food on their table, the clothes on their backs and the roof above their heads were matters for their own hard work, and each decided for himself how well to provide. The idea that government might have a responsibility in these directions would have been regarded as preposterous at best, more certainly as a hideous intrusion. There was a suspicion that the government was running the country badly and that somehow the poor price for beef was a consequence, but no one was quite sure what running the country really amounted to and the connection with individual hard luck was too remote for anyone to blame their misfortunes on anything other than capricious fate or their own bad management.

There was no theft, no violence, no chiselling, no cheating. Delinquency was not even a word in the local vocabulary. Men left their doors unlocked and their outfits unguarded, using each other's meadow cabins and equipment if the need arose. There was no by your leave, only a scrupulous leaving of whatever you used in just the state you'd found it.

As for young people getting into trouble, there wasn't time for it. The vital connection between the hard work of each passing day and the food on the table was so predominant a fact of survival that a child hardly paused for breath before picking up his share. Arne could not remember his first day's work but at twelve years he put in ten hours a day through the haying season, every day the sun shone.

Arne did well at school. He shared with others in the valley the necessity of riding horseback several miles to school every day. But there must have been something extra in favor of himself and his brothers and sisters for they were the one family in the valley to see the whole pack—his father's ungenerous term—through high school. This meant boarding in Williams Lake after the eighth grade and somewhere between then and the one year he spent in university Arne found that the extra was his mother.

She'd come into the valley as a school teacher and stayed to marry Bill Saunders and raise his "pack." She didn't grudge the life. Like Bill she believed in it. But she believed also, she explained long after to Arne, in choices, and choices came with knowing how to use your head. She appreciated the value of the ranch for that purpose but there were other disciplines to be found in books. She laid her mind to seeing her children through high school one by one and Bill Saunders never doubted the worth of it. He hadn't really counted on owning a pick-up truck anyway.

The ranch would have been squeezed a little harder to see

Arne through university if he'd wanted it but notwithstanding how easily it all came to him, books and scholarship were dull. He had liked the active life of the ranch, agreeing with his father that it was more fun than a trip to town to chase wild horses off Peavine Mountain or hitch a bronc to a hay mower on a boggy meadow.

So he had quit with the first year under his belt and in retrospect he hadn't regretted it. He'd missed a point here and there in Civil Service promotion competitions on account of it but he'd had a fistful of fun in the balance, so what the hell?

Arne stayed on the ranch till his next two brothers had their high school then, realizing the ranch couldn't absorb them all, he'd struck out on his own. He made big money laboring in sawmills, then spent it as quickly in weekends in the town. A little ashamed of that he then saved enough to buy a pick-up truck. With this he travelled around the province for the best part of three years, working on larger ranches much of the time, here and there a sawmill and once on a construction crew building a smelter on a tidal inlet on the north coast.

Then for two more years he contracted haying at a price per ton and fencing at a price by the mile for one of the larger ranches back in his home valley. He gathered a little equipment, hired a small crew, and worked to beat hell, pushing his crew as hard as he pushed himself.

He made it pay and he enjoyed it enough, but one drizzly day when he couldn't hay on account of the rain he came to the realization that he had no mind to do this for the rest of his life, and the days for chewing a ranch out of the bush the way his father had done were gone. The land for doing it with was all taken up, and if you had enough money to buy in, why hell, you'd have enough money you wouldn't have to.

Which put Arne to taking stock and he realized he was half fitted for a lot of things and well fitted for none. He could ride a horse and work stock, put up hay and build fence. Or he could run a gypo sawmill, rough carpenter a house, run a level on an irrigation ditch and build a half decent bridge on a side road. He knew how to mix concrete and trowel it to a fine finish and he could use a compass to do a traverse. He could keep a simple set of books and he'd written some fair to middling essays in university. He could run a crew and talk a banker into a short-term loan. He could butcher a steer and trap muskrats.

Mostly, he could work. He was a regular bear for work. But apart from that he was just a half-educated, regular Canadian boy who'd come out of the backwoods into an age with a mania for specialization and he didn't have the first idea what to do.

Going back to university to study for a profession was more than he cared to face. Concentrating on one trade out of all that he had turned his hand to, to carpenter or to work cement, solely without diversion, so as to extract from it a tradesman's pay, attracted him even less.

It was facing his own dilemma that brought him to thinking in more depth than before, about the Indian people he had known.

There were no occupied reserves in the valley. There was one small reserve on a lake beyond the farthest meadows of the ranch and when the fish came out of the lake to the creek to spawn, a family of Indians camped there to smoke a substantial catch.

Others travelled from time to time through the valley in wagons drawn by scrawny teams with saddle horses led behind and the wagon a jumble of kids and outfit. Sometimes a family would camp by the ranch and the man and maybe an older boy would ask for work for a few days, never more than a week or two, and Bill Saunders always agreed to it. He asserted he didn't know why they lived so hand to mouth but if a few days work would help he didn't mind and he paid them going wages. They were the only outside help he ever hired and he couldn't really afford it. But they never stayed after they had a few dollars coming, so it was no burden to the ranch.

Then Arne had worked alongside many Indian men his own age during the time he had spent on the larger ranches, and after that he had hired them in his own contracting camps. He'd come to know their women a little and if the truth ever got out, in fact, he'd gone on a bit of a toot with one older man he'd come to like rather more than most.

They'd been working together on a ranch in the Nicola Valley, and with the haying done and the crew laid off, he had decided to drive to Kamloops to look for work in the bush for the winter.

The old man, Charlie he was called and Arne never knew his other name, came with him and when they got to town Arne asked the old man what he'd like to do.

"Oh, just let me off any place. Maybe I see some people I know, I go with them."

"Well, aren't you gonna have a drink or something? We been dry up on that haystack for a month."

Charlie responded with the shy grin he had and said he wasn't supposed to drink, and Arne had paid so little attention to the business about liquor and Indians he didn't know what his friend was getting at.

"What d'ya mean, ya not supposed to?" Arne habitually fell into inferior pronunciation in the company of others who patched their English together the hard way.

"Us Indians, 'gainst the law for us to drink."

It was before even the beer parlors were open to them and suddenly Arne realized his mistake. In his shame at discomforting the old man he became embarrassed, then angry. "Well, by God, I'm gonna drink and if I'm gonna drink, you're gonna drink."

The upshot was that Arne dropped Charlie off then fetched a handsome supply of beer plus one bottle of expensive whisky. Then he rendezvoused with his friend and they drove to a side road where they hid the truck and themselves in the brush and got down to some serious drinking.

Arne was never clear in his memory afterward, but he knew they'd gone into town again that night, and for the next two days, perhaps three, they'd done considerable going about looking up friends Charlie knew on the reserve on the north side of the river, and drinking in great secrecy and in substantial quantities, saying maudlin things about the way white men and Indians ought to treat one another more like people.

Looking back from the wet days of that later haying season, it seemed to Arne the Indians were in much the same fix he found himself, except worse. They cowboyed a little or kept a few cows on the reserve. Some worked in sawmills sporadically, but from what he could see of it they had no enthusiasm for anything they saw around them. Born to one kind of life they faced another and found it alien. Arne had been born to the life of a pioneer rancher, but ranching was long out of the pioneering stage now. He could understand, he thought, a people with serious doubts about where they were going to fit in.

It had been a long wet haying season with plenty of time for thinking and by the end of it Arne had reached a tentative decision. When the last stack was up and measured and his crew paid off and disbanded he went into Williams Lake to the Indian Affairs office to discover what chance there was that one itinerant ranch hand with a year of university might make a career of helping a whole lot of itinerant ranch hands with maybe not even high school.

12

I t had been a little startling at the time, the rapidity with which Arne Saunders found himself made into a federal civil servant. Even looking back fifteen years later when he was superintendent of the Yucla–Davis Bay Indian Agency on British Columbia's ragged coast line, he was still astonished at how quickly it had all happened.

Yes, the Indian Affairs Branch had field positions in programs to help Indian people fit into modern society. No, a university degree or any particular specialization wasn't necessary. But you needed lots of common sense and some experience in farming, ranching or fishing. Well, because Indians lived where it would be most natural for them to farm or ranch in the interior or fish on the coast. Show them how it's done, you see. And experience in house construction would help too. The branch builds houses for Indians.

Any current openings? Yes, a vacancy at Kamloops is being advertised right now. Here's the poster. You get an application form at the post office and fill it out, then send it to the Civil Service Commission in Vancouver. Be sure to tell them about your experience in ranching and mention the construction job too. And any positions of responsibility. You did a small contracting business in ranch work? Well, you mention that.

So Arne fetched the form from the post office and spent a few hours resurrecting the bent he'd had for English composition. When he was done he had mildly surprised himself—how impressive he made it all sound! He stressed the part about working with Indian men and hiring them in his own crews. He left out the time in Kamloops with Charlie and decided that if he did get the job and bumped into Charlie sometime, he'd have to ask forgiveness for not being so sporting as before. It seemed evident that his new role wouldn't accommodate a booze-up with one of the boys.

The application was acknowledged and in time Arne was called for an interview. This went well, Arne thought. Most of the questions focused on the practical aspects of ranch work and he had thoughtful answers.

He had expected more penetration into what was after all a fearfully limited experience of the people themselves for someone now offering to make a life's work of solving their problems, but his brief association with a few individuals seemed in some way to be sufficient.

He heard nothing for several weeks during which he went home to help his father do some riding. He'd have to find a job in the logging camps for the winter if the application and the interview led to nothing, but he couldn't commit himself to anything until he knew.

Then a short letter came in the mail offering him the job.

And Arne Saunders, born of people whose fundamental attitude toward all government, politicians and civil servants alike, was one of distrust and varying degrees of contempt, buckled on the studded clasp of ultimate security and began the long haul down the years to a government pension.

Less than a year later he discovered that one Stella Mitchell, daughter of a neighboring rancher, had come to Kamloops to work in the telephone exchange. He found that she had somehow acquired all manner of charms that had been, Arne thought, singularly lacking when with pug nose and freckle face she had driven a hefty team of blacks hitched to a mower around the long reach of her father's hay fields.

He married her, quickly, before she changed back into that kid with the pug nose, he said. In short order they had two girls.

Whereupon Arne would look at the face in the mirror when he shaved in the morning, shake his head and say softly to himself: "You son-of-a-gun, you sure lucky you got a steady job. How'n hell did it happen to you anyway?"

13

Arne did not regret that he had chosen this work. Because the whole range of relationships a non-Indian citizen might have with a multitude of departments and agencies were for Indian people concentrated in one branch, the job never suffered two days alike.

He issued relief to people unable to make a living by employment or farming on the reserve; he inspected logging operations carried out by Indians under permit from the Agency office; he sorted out land disputes and recorded the settlements on careful sketches based on chain and compass traverse; he administered estates; he supervised fencing and ditching works; he negotiated with non-Indian farmers and ranchers the terms on which a particular band might lease out a piece of the reserve for which it had no immediate use itself.

He met with the band councils, at first under the supervision of his superintendent but later on his own, to explain to them the decisions they must reach: to accept or reject an application to lease, to allot or not a parcel of land in the reserve for the use of an individual band member, to budget the expenditures which would be suitable from their band funds held in trust in Ottawa, to accept or not compensation allowed for a road right-of-way crossing the reserve, to admit or not a member of another band wishing to transfer in.

Much of his work was in house construction. Because the Indian people generally had very limited incomes and no means of borrowing because they could not mortgage their land, the Branch appropriated increasing sums annually for the construction and repair of houses. They were low cost, minimum standard houses but they offered shelter to many people presently without it, and when a family took an interest in doing a little on their own, the house could be made into a pleasant little home, far more than mere shelter. On the other hand they could be and often were reduced to a shambles in two or three years by families with no idea whatever how to keep them up.

Working from drawings and material lists supplied by the engineering section in the regional office in Vancouver, Arne selected houses to suit the sizes of the families, requisitioned material and hired the necessary tradesmen to build the dwellings. He talked with the families about siting the houses and asked for their help during construction so that the limited money would go as far as possible. There was little choice of styles outside of how many bedrooms, and that question was answered by the size of the family. It was just impossible to have variety; the need for economy dictated that the houses had to be standardized. They came cheaper that way.

The Branch operated day schools on the reserves and one large residential school at Kamloops. Getting the youngsters from the broken homes and from the outlying places where there was no day school into the residential school in the fall was time consuming and the last of them were never in until well into October; still, that wasn't half so time consuming as looking up the little rascals who were supposed to but almost daily simply didn't attend the day school on the reserve.

Then, although the supervision of the teaching side at the day schools was done by a professional inspector working out of the regional office, Arne had to see to maintenance and material supply: repaint the classrooms, requisition fuel, meet the emergency when a power plant broke down.

The people on the reserves assigned him soon began to refer to him as the agent although that term had been out of official use for some years. Properly, the man in charge of the Indian Agency was called the superintendent and Arne's title was Agency assistant.

But of more significance than how they referred to him was how the people came to rely on him.

If they had trouble with the irrigation works, they'd call him. If the bull the branch provided to service their few head of breeding cows got sick, they'd ask him what to do. When he visited the reserve, they'd ask his advice on how to fix the sag in the foundation of the house or, more simply, if maybe he could fix it. In the spring they'd ask him for garden seed and in the fall they'd want a few lengths of pipe for the heater. A man whose wife had left with another would want Arne to get her back, a mother with an errant daughter needed him to "smarten her up."

He was forever filling out a pension application or a form for family allowances. Sometimes, encouragingly, he could help an older youngster who wanted to take training in a vocational school to complete an application for financial assistance from the Branch as well as the application to the school.

Occasionally he seemed at cross purposes with the people. When he was most anxious to get them cleaning up around their houses, they seemed more anxious to see if he had any old donated clothing in the warehouse at the back of the office.

When he would be preoccupied with getting a drilling rig backed into a ravine to drill a well for a couple of new houses, they would want to know how come the Agency didn't have any alfalfa seed this year.

But this didn't distress him. He could see he was of use to them and if their sense of priorities conflicted with his occasionally, it was hardly to be worried about.

He did worry at times, however, about the extent to which he was making decisions in areas where more normally someone with professional qualifications ought to have been in charge.

Social assistance in the non-Indian community was administered by people preferably with a degree in social work, never with less than in-service training experience and the close supervision of a professional. Where children were neglected by their parents, the provincial service did come into the reserves, because in the absence of protection legislation in the Indian Act the provincial legislation was deemed to apply. But invariably it was through Arne's intervention that a provincial worker came in; as often as not it was his judgment that led the case to court, his evidence that resulted in committal of the child to the care of the superintendent of child welfare for the province.

He was not a trained forester and yet the real management

of timber lands on the reserves fell to him; he was not a qualified agronomist yet the direct use and the leasing for revenue of the agricultural lands rested on his decision; he was not an engineer yet the decisions in laying out house sites and solving construction problems were made at his desk.

He was not a qualified counsellor yet it was by his interest and direct advice that here and there a youngster who had given up at school found his way back into some useful training.

There was of course an engineering section in the regional office, and the project engineers came out to design and construct the major works in irrigation and roads and larger buildings such as schools. And there were professional people in education at the regional office to whom the teaching staffs reported.

But these professional people were few in number and spread thin; for much of the work they could not be available and it was often a case of make your own decision or do without.

The Agency superintendent helped Arne a good deal at first. But he was an older man, mainly occupied in waiting for his retirement, and it became apparent to them both that Arne's common sense was as good as his. To give him credit, he left Arne free to do the job once he'd given Arne what he could offer.

So Arne began picking brains. Methodically, he tracked down sources of help: the Dominion Range Station, specializing in grassland management, the provincial district agriculturist, the Water Rights Branch, the district forest ranger, the social work supervisor, the high school counsellor.

When he had sorted out who was willing to help, he immersed himself in their fields, drilling them for hours on the direct application of their particular science, reading the periodicals and pamphlets they gave him, persuading them out into the back corners of reserves to tell him what they would do with one of his problems if it were theirs.

Foresters inspected the logging operations and crop specialists looked at his leasing programs. A social work supervisor criticized his severity in administration of social assistance and a water rights engineer, who happened to have specialized in drainage problems, told him how he could salvage a piece of sour bottom land.

When he could talk back to people in their own disciplines he began to feel adequate.

"Damn it, Arne, you're exhausting. I work at my job all day. I don't want to argue about it all night."

"Have another beer. I'm still not convinced that a residential school isn't better than a broken home and a drunken mother."

Sometimes this picking of brains cost him a lot of beer.

14

Arne grew competent in the language of all the disciplines of his work, and more than once he was embarrassed to be asked what he had taken at university. His reply that he hadn't gone brought an awkward silence he found difficult to breach. His right of debate seemed taken away.

But this same facility showed in his reports and stood him well before rating boards in promotion competitions. Within two years he went to another Agency in the interior as an assistant at the next grade; within two more he became superintendent of a small Agency in the southeast part of the province.

He grew competent in the ways of a junior government administrator.

He mastered the bookkeeping system by which the Agency accounted for the cash it handled. If his clerk couldn't balance at month end he lost little time isolating the error.

He understood the filing system and its significance in good management. Without becoming preoccupied with records for their own sake, he insisted on highly logical filing so that when he dealt with any subject everything pertinent was before him and nothing incoming or outgoing could be lost.

He developed easily maintained costing systems, producing accurate and well-supported estimates for the ensuing year's operations.

He was restive about the endless reports to the regional office but having made his complaints he filed them promptly and wrote them well. He doubted that they were read but he made them worth reading.

He controlled his budget with care and though he overspent regularly in some activities he had always a soundly documented reason for so doing.

A little ruefully, he realized that he had also acquired a technique for winning his differences with the Branch. With hard argument and an occasional touch of contrition, with indignation tempered by moments of compassion for the burdens of Region, with self-effacement at some times and utter conceit at others, he won the extra dollars for a road he wanted to build, approval of a band council's budget to which a faceless name in headquarters objected, or passage of an account most offensive to the clerks of the Treasury.

Indeed, a bright and promising career lay before him, and in his rasher moments he had been cautioned not to put it in jeopardy by being so intemperately outspoken.

It was interesting that others thought of it, for he rarely did himself.

What grew to obsess him wholly was that the program he managed so diligently did, or appeared to do, so damn little about the grief of Indians.

It was a long time before he first acknowledged just how bad life was on the reserves. He had a great natural optimism about what could be accomplished through hard work. He assumed that others shared it and that even in the seemingly indolent it waited below the surface only needing to be kindled. Since he could himself have done so much had he the chances available to most of the people, he anticipated from others the results he could expect of himself. If they all just worked at it—the Indians and himself everything would be prosperous in so short a while.

Arne worked, relentlessly.

But nothing changed. He was never sure just when the turning point was reached, but afterward he always remembered a day when he had stood in the midst of a field of weeds and cursed under the hot sun every Indian on whom he'd ever laid eyes and every one he hadn't, in an avalanche of frustration with a whole entire race.

The field of weeds belonged to a man for whom he had gone the whole way. He'd needed a house and Arne had got it for him, though God knows he might have done a lot more to get it on his own. But Arne had rationalized the man's wasteful ways and his drinking, certain that the new house would encourage him. They had talked about the drinking problem and the fellow was sincere, you could tell that.

His wife had wanted the children home from residence to go to the day school and the new house made it possible. She had given her earnest word that they would attend without fail.

The man worked seasonally in a logging operation on a piecework basis. Arne had intervened when the operator had given up employing him on a regular shift because of his drinking. Arne invested several evenings in developing the idea that some men can't help their drinking and that employers, as part of their social responsibility, must make some work available in which regular attendance on a shift isn't necessary. So a corner of the timber stand was set aside in which the man could fall and buck and skid with his horses to a landing the light logs that grew there.

The team wasn't up to much, a pair of old geldings left by his uncle, but it would do. But horses must be wintered and Arne persuaded the band council to let the man use the band-owned tractor to break the field behind his house, and Arne brought him the seed to start the alfalfa with a nurse crop of oats.

Everything had gone well. The logging provided a living and the house, though poorly kept, provided shelter. The children were in the day school although their attendance hadn't been quite what it should, and the land had been broken.

Arne worried a little that he had been too much a factor, that perhaps the family's heart wasn't in it and they had only responded out of deference to himself. So he asked them about that, and they gave him every assurance. He was struck by the intelligent way they appreciated their own situation. And they did have a wonderful opportunity. The logging could be made to pay much better than wages in the mill, and it would still leave time for growing feed for the horses and a cash crop of hay besides. There was plenty of land under irrigation and the council had agreed to let him have all he could work. Without land tax or income tax to pay from the earnings, since no taxes applied on the reserve, the part-time farming could be tidily profitable.

Arne left the seed with a feeling of gratitude to people who would try so hard for their own betterment.

He saw and heard nothing for the next several weeks and then suffered a deluge of dismal tidings.

The children had missed virtually all of the last two months of school and had failed their year because of it.

The man had delivered exactly thirty-eight dollars and forty cents worth of logs to the landing in that same time.

He had borrowed the band tractor again to seed in the crop—which he could have done with his horses. But instead of cropping in, he had sold the seed and used the tractor to go into town, where he had stayed drunk for a week.

Beside all this, it came out that he had not broken the land himself in the first place. He had hired a non-Indian farmer to do the work on promise of a share of the hay in the fall, and had used the band tractor at that time to skid in a rush all the close logs immediately around the landing to make some quick cash.

Arne went to see him, determined to reserve judgment until he had the other side of the story. But he found the man and his wife drunk, the children clad in rags, no food in the house, the house itself indescribably filthy, half the windows broken, and the field, which should have been rich in green, waving oat tops, solid in weeds.

The ancient geldings stood idly in the corner of it, flicking flies with their tails.

Arne said nothing to the couple. He only walked into the field to see if somewhere beneath the weeds there might not be the signs of perhaps a late sowing of the seed and of course there wasn't. The worst was true.

And he took a handful of the rich earth from which any man might easily make harvest in all the years of his life, rich earth that would give bounty in fair exchange for honest toil, and he crumbled it in his fingers, letting it fall in fine granules back to the ground. *The hardest goddamned people on earth to help.*

15

There had followed a time of cynicism in which Arne berated himself for having been so starry-eyed and unrealistic about the hard facts of how the people lived.

With few exceptions (so few that on some reserves there were none), they lived in degradation and waste.

They drank. Man and woman, they drank. Every damn chance they got, they drank. On family allowance day they crowded the beer parlors in the towns and drank till they were insensible. Between times they home-brewed and drank the rank, yeasty, rotgut while it was still bubbling in fermentation. And as they drank it went on fermenting in their stomachs until they were dog sick and drunk at the same time. And still they forced it down, even while they threw up on it.

For the sake of the children, they were issued with social assistance and they drank that if they got it in cash. So Arne issued food vouchers, and in the beer parlors on relief day you could buy for a couple of dollars a box of groceries intended to last a family a week; two dollars—ten glasses of beer.

Their houses were squalid and filthy, so bad it turned your stomach to walk in. You had to force from your mind the fact that people prepared food and ate it in such places. In a matter of months new houses were reduced to the same shambles as the old. They were warmer and they kept the rain out, but for sanitation they were the same germ-ridden hovels the people had come out of when the new houses were built. The children fared worse than anyone. With rags on their backs—new clothing purchased by the Agency somehow became rags in a matter of days—they hustled their living by competing furtively with the adults for what little food did from time to time come into their houses, and by begging continually from the old people who had pensions.

Sometimes whole villages lived on the food of the old people, for the old people not only had pensions which they did spend on food but they also preserved the food of their ancestors, the dried fish and meat and berries and roots on which once the people had survived. And the old people suffered the burden of feeding the whole village from their pensions and their toil in the food-making season because they had no choice. Sometimes the younger people were even more direct about it; they simply came at pension time and took the checks.

And with the drinking came the violence. Men in gangs set upon individuals, leaving them bleeding and broken. Men turned on their wives, and life for many women became a continual round of beatings and threats of beatings. One man used a short piece of two-by-four to respond to his wife's pregnancies, which he no longer wanted. The method was effective.

Their children came back into residence after the summer not only with dirt and parasites but with bruises and half-healed scars as well.

They had no interest in anything, however useful to them, that required the least effort. They wouldn't take employment, they wouldn't work their fields, they wouldn't care for livestock, they wouldn't, save for the old people among them, preserve the Indian foods. They wouldn't screw a hinge back on a door, nor nail down a loose board. They'd stuff rags in broken windows, but only after the cold crept in. They wouldn't fetch wood until the fire was out, nor draw water until thirst was on them.

The houses Arne built deteriorated shamefully. The schools he maintained were only half attended. The irrigation works he installed put land in production that was then leased out to white men, with the rentals squandered. The seed he provided was wasted or bootlegged. The wells he drilled were contaminated by children defecating in the well houses while the parents looked on indifferently.

The use of the social assistance he issued to keep people alive in spite of themselves became the subject of a continual contest between himself and the people. They wanted to convert it somehow to drink; he insisted they damn well use it for food and essentials.

Band councils were often a farce. They were frequently elected in indifference, knowing little and caring less what their responsibilities might be. They went through the formalities of their work under Arne's persuasion while he carried out all the substance of it.

When Arne met with the criticism that the Indians didn't do anything for themselves because the government was doing it all for them, he all but wept with frustration. If only the critics knew the hours he had toiled to extract just a fragment of response from the people themselves to their own needs. But you couldn't explain. If Arne didn't build houses for them, there would be no houses. If he didn't see to the irrigation works, there would be no land under ditch at all. If he didn't continually keep his field men on truancy, the children would never be in school. If he didn't issue social assistance, there would be nothing for the children to eat.

It wasn't because the government did these things that the people didn't. It was because the people wouldn't do them, or even make half a try at it, that the government had to.

It was all so damnably hopeless.

16

T hose had been difficult days for Arne. He had seriously thought of quitting, but his fundamental reaction to work harder the tougher the job became had prevented it.

Once more a time came which, in retrospect, he recognized as a turning point in his own attitudes.

The seeds had been in him all along, of course. However harsh his own judgments were, he still found himself defending Indian people against the harshness of others.

He once turned in rage on a delegation of white parents who had come to his office to protest against the dirt and the lice which they feared would rub off on their children in a classroom where, for the first time, some children from a neighboring reserve had been enrolled.

"Look, what in hell do you expect? That we're going to remodel these people into nice, clean-smelling, white middle-class property-worshippers before we ask you to *accept* them?

"Can't you realize that the grandparents, just the living grand-parents, the parents of the parents of those kids were a nomadic bunch of people who moved around here hunting and fishing and digging up roots before we fenced the place up, and they just didn't have any use for our kind of sanitation?

"They didn't have any use for just about everything we demand of them. They didn't have clocks and dull bloody jobs and money and people to look down their noses at them because they weren't clean and white and...and *fashionable*.

"You know how they lived? It was a tough life, but it worked. They had all kinds of ingenious ways to get food with simple tools they made with their bare hands. They moved their camps with the seasons so they'd be in the right place for a particular food. They got in time with their environment and they didn't impose any artificial system of minutes and hours and days of the week on it. They ate when they were hungry, if there was anything to eat, and they slept when they were tired, and got up when they were rested.

"I'm not saying it was a *good* way of life or that our own is a *bad* one. It's senseless to make judgments like that about a way of life. People are born to a way of life and it works for them for better or worse.

"But you know what they didn't have? They didn't have houses in fixed places where you couldn't move on to a fresh place when that one got dirty. They didn't have any need for our kind of cleanliness. I understand we didn't either, back in the Middle Ages. The lord of the manor himself smelled like an athlete's undershirt.

"And they didn't have anything necessary to survival that involved boredom in fixed quantities eight hours a day, five days a week, fifty weeks a year, every year of your life.

"And they weren't farmers. But we can't understand why they won't farm. Why the hell should they farm? The only reason we think they should farm is we're so muddle-headed ourselves we think anybody who can't hack it in some clean-handed job somewhere can at least go farming.

"They didn't have booze either. And they haven't had a few thousand years to get used to upsetting their systems with alcohol the way we have and develop a whole framework of customs around drinking so they know how to do it in an *acceptable* way. They just do it plain and it wipes out whatever's left of their grip on themselves.

"Look, I don't know what it's like to be an Indian, but it must be a pretty confusing and dismal business. I'm not sure what Indian people value, if they value anything any more, but they certainly haven't had the chance to learn to value all the things that *you* value. And I guess I haven't really said anything that means very much, except I can say this: if we're going to be any use to Indians we're going to have to accept them as they are, not as we'd like them to be. And if right now they are in one hell of a confused mess, and part of that is dirt and lice, then we're going to accept them, dirt and lice in the bargain.

"Who in that classroom has everything going for him and who hasn't, your kids or the Indian kids? Who's the middle-class school system geared for? Whose language are the books written in? Whose parents can help them with their homework? Which kids know they can go to the teacher if they're in trouble? Hell, for those Indian kids, that white middle-class school teacher and the system she represents *is* the trouble.

"So you come in here to defend your kids against some dirt and lice stuck to an Indian kid. Well, I'm here to defend that Indian kid. Somehow he has to tough it out in that place until he, or his kids, or his kids' kids, get something out of it because whether it's fair or not the only way to hack it now is our way. We've destroyed his way."

The outburst had drained him. He hadn't been conscious that he had so much to say in defense of the people and he had gone on so long that when he stopped and there was a silence, he had nothing more to tide it over.

One of the women in the group finally dispelled it. "I'm sorry Mr. Saunders. We hadn't thought of that side of it. You see, I've never even *seen* lice and when my boy told me one of the Indian children had to be...well, deloused, I checked with the nurse and found it was true. Honestly, it shocked me. You make it sound horrid of us to be worried about our own children but I really don't know what I'll *do* if my two come home with lice. Especially my little girl."

Arne looked at her directly and grinned. "Delouse them," he

said, and some of the sudden warmth he felt for her in her bewilderment must have got through. Her hands went up to her face and she stifled a startled laugh.

"All right," she said. "I will. I'll ask the nurse." With that the delegation left and Arne turned to the window to look out while he mused a little at his own outburst. On the street below a drunk Indian lurched along the sidewalk and in a moment the police van pulled up. Two officers stepped out and with no difficulty put the unresisting man in the back, then pulled away. Section 94(b) Indian Act, intoxicated off a reserve. Ten dollars or ten days. Next case.

Next case, indeed. You're a case yourself, Arne Saunders. You get so fed up with Indian people you could spit, and then you blow off at a white man if he suggests they might be a little lazy or a little dirty or a little wasteful of their substance—which is pretty much why you get fed up with them yourself.

But it was somewhere out of that dilemma that Arne found the middle ground that helped him to go on trying to help. He explained it to himself later that he quit pretending that Indians by and large were just as successful as anybody else because obviously by and large they weren't. By and large that was pretty easily understood, because it was in someone else's world and not their own that success now had to be accomplished.

Following on that, he escaped the discomfort of his earlier judgment that by and large Indians weren't as good as other people, because in fact good and bad didn't enter into it. It was really just whether people were fortunate enough to understand their situation so that they could be effective in it or unfortunate enough to be so confused by it they could only fail.

Within this framework he found it entirely possible and indeed logical to extend to people responsibility for the consequences of their own actions; not for the antecedents which landed them in the situation, but certainly for the immediate consequences of a specific action.

"Okay, Charlie, look at it this way. If you *want* to have some potatoes in the root house this fall, you have to seed 'em in now and you have to fuss with 'em a bit this summer. If you *want* dry wood next winter, you have to cut it now. It's your choice so you make it. But don't come to me with a long story about your hard luck if you don't have spuds and firewood when you need 'em, because you and I both know you can do something about it right now if you want to. All right?"

"Okay, Mr. Saunders. You betcha."

Well, there wouldn't be any spuds or dry firewood and Charlie still had a long story about hard luck, but Arne didn't accept him any less on account of it.

And Arne found he'd been much too inclined to generalize about the people. While it was true that all the unhappy failings—the drinking and the squalor, the child neglect and the wife beating, the continual need for social allowance followed by the squandering of it, the abuse of the dwelling place—that all these occurred with alarming frequency throughout the reserves, and in some reserves in every family, they did not happen with everyone everywhere.

There were those people and sometimes groups of people where sensible, productive lives were lived, where men still knew that, whatever the circumstances unwitting fate delivered him into, it rested with a man if he was to do well and not with an agent of government; it rested with a man if he was to make happiness for his children, take care of his house, gather a few belongings by which to make his life easier and preserve his own substance. Some men might not have it in them to make these things happen, but if they were to happen at all, it had to come from the man himself.

Government could not make them happen. Arne learned this from a few wise people who had somehow bridged two worlds, living successfully by the universal standard that a man must carry himself, not look to others to be carried. These men had no less and no more external opportunity than any of the others. They shared the same reserves, they had access to the same employments, they had to resist the same temptations.

They were the people who benefited from the Branch's programs—who borrowed from the loan fund and paid it back, who used the housing subsidy and added to it for a more substantial dwelling, who kept cows to be serviced by the government bull, who expanded their crops with branch-supplied seed, who made use of the tractor bought from band funds.

And the irony was *that they would have succeeded just as well without any of the Branch's help,* because it was in them.

And the others would never succeed, no matter how much help the Branch tried to give, because it was not in them.

In the quiet of a harvest twilight Arne sat with an old man looking over the corner of the reserve which had prospered many years under this one's diligent use, and he listened to the soft words spoken to him in great kindness.

"You try hard, Mr. Saunders. I know you try hard.

"But you not gonna change them people, Mr. Saunders.

"You take that Charlie Willie. Long time back his dad an' my dad, they both have a place on other side of the river, little places side by side. They livin' some old way, makin' dry meat and the old women diggin' roots an' dryin' berries. They live some new way too. They growin' hay an' they got a few cows.

"They makin' out okay. Indian agent comes maybe once a year them days. Me and Charlie about same age an' we don't go to school but mission priest comes once in a while, an' he shows us enough we can read and write just a little bit.

"But my dad, he makin' us work. If us kids don't want to work for old man, he's sendin' us to dig roots with them women. Well, we don't want woman's work so we workin' for old man. It gets so hot we makin' that hay, I don't know how I'm gonna stand it till sun goes down. No machinery then. We makin' it all by hand. God, he's hot in that hay field. All summer we makin' hay like that. Since small boy every summer.

"But Charlie, his old man not makin' him work. I guess he don't have to make him work to get by. Not too hard to get by them days. Maybe my old man don't have to make us work to get by, but he's makin' us work anyway.

"Charlie, he's growin' up an' he's never have to work. He's livin' off his old people an' finally them old people die an' Charlie he's sell all the stuff, an' one day he's got nothin' left, only now he's got his own woman an' kids.

"Well, you know Charlie now. He's livin' in that shack an' he's drinkin' an' his boys all grown up an' they drinkin', an' some of them got kids now too an' them kids in trouble all the time.

"They a big bunch now, them Willies, must be a couple dozen

altogether now an' not a good one in the bunch. Probably you givin' 'em relief so them kids not starvin'.

"But you not gonna change 'em, Mr. Saunders. You sendin' those kids to school an' you buildin' 'em new houses, but you not gonna change 'em.

"I try one time, you know. I take that boy, Jackie. I bring him here an' I tell him, you work for me an' I going to help you get started. So I pay him few dollars an' I show him everything how to do it. Then I help him fence up that place used to be his gran'dad's an' I lend him my tractor an' stuff, an' he gets that place all seeded in. An' still he's workin' for me. He's not much good an' he's only workin' when I'm right with him, but I say to myself, he's gonna be all right when he gets used to it.

"So he gets a little hay off that place an' I give him few cows for part of his wages and I tell him, you run those cows same time you workin' for me an' maybe few years you got enough, you be on you own.

"Well, it don't work. One day he's don't show up for few weeks, an' I find out he's sold them cows an' stay drunk in town till it's all gone and he's lease that hay land to white man an' he drinks whatever he gets for rent.

"Worst part, he don't like me any more. He spreads bad word about me an' he lookin' the other way when I see him in town.

"An' all them Willie boys, they given' me trouble. They don't got a damn thing of they own so they think I'm an old son-of-a-bitch cause I got a few stuff. Well, only reason I got a few stuff is I work for it an' save for it an' pay for it. Them boys got nothin' cause they don't work for nothin'. But still they think I'm somehow buggerin' them up cause I got a few stuff an' they tryin' to wreck what I got. They leavin' the gate down so my cows gets on the track an' hit by train, they takin' parts off my machines, even they got no machines themselves to use it on. My truck breaks down one day by their place an' I get a ride home an' go back next day to fix it an' they takin' everything off it. I go into their place an' find all that stuff an' I don't go to police, I just takin' it back an' all that time, they swearin' at me.

"But you can't blame 'em you know. Even that old man never teach that boy to work, he don't understand the trouble he's startin'. He thinks it's okay, they gettin' by without that boy workin' so no need for that boy to work. He can work when he grows up, he figures.

"But you can't blame you self either, Mr. Saunders. It not your fault them Willies all haywire an' you not gonna change 'em.

"I hear some white men in meetin' sometime, he says it's white man's fault that Indian's all poor an' don't got nothin' an' don't got job an' drinkin' all the time.

"Well, white man brings big change all right an' some Indian, he don't take that big change, I guess. But no white man make that Willie outfit live like that. He got same chance as me, but he don't use it. Maybe it not his fault, but I don't think it anybody else fault.

"I gonna tell you. It's same for white man and same for Indian. It's same in old days an' it's same now. If you gonna live an' you gonna eat and have little stuff to make you life, you got to work for it an' then you got to hang on to what you get an' not throw it away.

"Some people came here one time an' hold meetin' in town. I like meetin' in town. Makes me think about things, so I go to meetin' when I hear 'bout it. Any kind meetin', it don't matter.

"Well, these guys sayin' there is all kinds machines now an' people don't got to work no more. Just the government should give everybody money to get what he wants, an' them machines they doin' all the work.

"But I can't figure that. How the hell any machine gonna look after my cows an' know when to put up my hay when I just sittin' here livin' on that money the government gonna give me?

"Sure, machines is big help. That hay baler, that's great rig. Makes my work lots easier than old days when I makin' hay by hand. But still I got to work.

"I tell you what it's like. It's this way. I have hard time to explain it but I understand it myself. Maybe they is a few people got enough money they can live without workin'. Maybe he's lucky his dad makes lots an' leaves it to him and he's got to be lucky enough it don't ruin him an' make him like those Willies.

"But that's only a few people. Some say it isn't right, nobody should have a bunch of money like that, so much he don't got to work. Well, I don't think much about that cause it makes no difference how I got to get by. Nobody gonna leave me no money.

"So never mind about few people like that. What everybody got to remember is, we got to work if we goin' to live. Maybe we don't got to work hellishin' *hard* but we got to work. We got to find somethin' we can do and then we got to do it regular. An' we got to look after what we get for doin' it.

"Even old days, Indian got no job like workin' in sawmill but still he got to work at gettin' his different food an' makin' his camp an' fixin' hides. Otherwise he's gonna die. No relief in them days.

"Worst thing can happen to you is you don't learn to work like them Willies never learned to work or maybe you learn to work all right an' then you get some kind idea you don't *got* to work. Like you think he's a rich government an' he should look after you. Then you in trouble.

"I see some young white people in town now. They got long hair an' they kinda dirty an' you get close to 'em, they smelly. I think they in that kind trouble they think somebody should look after 'em, they don't got to work."

The sun was down and in the cool air that filled the valley the rich smell of the fresh-cut alfalfa gathered all around them. The old man fell silent for a long time, while Arne wondered if in his straightforward simplicity there wasn't more truth than in all the sophisticated sociology between the covers of important volumes.

Then a last few words: "So you got to remember, you not gonna change 'em. You got to look after 'em cause they can't make it on they own. But no use to blame anybody for it. We just got to look after 'em. Sure'n hell, it not your fault."

17

It was the administration of social assistance that crystallized all the conflicting philosophy into a hard, knotty and unremitting problem for Arne.

Excluding education and new construction, 30 per cent of his budget went into social assistance to provide the necessities of life to people who were unable or unwilling to provide for themselves. Apart from this, another 50 per cent went into direct payments to the province for maintenance of children who had had to be taken from their parents and, in the custody of the superintendent of child welfare, placed in foster homes. Inflation being what it was, these costs were now running at six dollars per child per day, including the cost of administration of the child protection service.

Arne had plenty of advice.

The Branch, as a policy, told its field service to administer social allowances at the scale and according to the practices of the province in which they were situated.

That was fair enough as far as it went, and it was a big improvement on an earlier and decidedly niggardly system of issuing rations that had hung over much too long from the last century.

Allowances to the unemployable were never a problem. A man prematurely old and unable to work but not due for pension yet, a widow with children, a youngster cared for by a relative and still attending school: these were easily decided, and Arne squeezed every cent the regulations allowed to provide not only for life, but dignity too. It was the able-bodied man, who was capable of taking up one of the available jobs but who persistently sought allowances instead, who created for Arne the dilemma that would not fall to easy solutions.

The philosophy of the province held that a man who seeks social allowance in preference to work has, at the least, a problem of adjustment to the industrial life. He may also lack skills to meet the increasing sophistication of the available employments, but even when the work is such that he can clearly do it, he must have an attitude problem with which he needs help. Otherwise, he wouldn't be seeking assistance.

Ideally, the social worker issues assistance sufficient for life and dignity then, through a casework relationship, helps the man to modify his attitudes so that he returns by his own choice to employment.

In reality, no one in the provincial service or Indian Affairs had time to change attitudes if, indeed, casework could change attitudes.

So the assistance was issued, according to provincial policy, and by and large it went on being issued.

Except that for Arne a torrent of his own attitudes came boiling up to interfere. He could not divest himself of the belief that a man had no damned right to be maintained by the community if there was work he could do by which to maintain himself.

Because other superintendents had either had less difficulty "buying" the policy or were more lenient because it was easier, or were merely more gullible when it came to hard luck stories, Arne continually found himself following where others had been doing what he could not go on doing himself.

A father of six children sat across the desk from him defying his authority to refuse assistance.

"By God, I'll write Ottawa. You see if I don't."

"Go ahead, Jimmy. I'll give you the director's address. But I won't give you social assistance. You're as capable of getting a job in the bush as anyone else."

"My kids got nothing to eat right now. Even I get a job, I don't get paid for two weeks."

"You get a job and as soon as you go to work I'll arrange for a couple of weeks' grub for the family. But first you get the job."

The door all but came off its hinges as Jimmy went out, but by noon the next day he had the job. He never came back, and he worked without layoff for the three years that Arne knew of before his next transfer took him away.

It wasn't always so easy. A man who hadn't worked for four years, and whose determination not to was as great as Arne's that he should, played the hunger of his children like trumps in a card game. There were four long months in which Arne parcelled out reducing amounts, just enough to keep the children from starvation but not enough to prevent their hunger, while he hammered the man's conscience with every weapon he could find.

"If you aren't man enough to do man's work, why don't you dig roots like the women? Or maybe you are not even an Indian any more and you can't find the roots. Ask your old mother, she'll help you."

Arne knew hatred when it was directed at him in silent, seething, monumental quantities. And he knew the hunger of little children.

But finally the man went to work. In two months he had more food in his house, his wife said, than they'd had for years. Within the year they had a washing machine and a new stove, and he had reduced his drinking to weekend binges.

Arne not only held out against the story that a man couldn't find a job, nobody'd hire an Indian any more, and the accompanying plea that there was not food in the house or that the family had had no income; he went sleuthing into the truth of all the stories told him in the appeal for assistance.

He went into cupboards and found provisions that people had denied existed; he went to the fish camps and saw the drying salmon; he went to the sawmills and verified that the jobs were there if men seriously wanted them; he went to the beer parlors to find there was money for drinking when it had been claimed there was none for food.

He called meetings in villages and laid everything on the line: "Look, I'm not here to tell you how to live. You can live the old way and put up the Indian foods, or you can live the new way and get a job. Or you can do some of both.

"And if someone is crippled or old or a widow, we'll issue all the assistance we can.

"But you guys that are young and strong and capable, you'd better make up your minds which way you're going to do it, because there is not going to be any handout for you.

"If you've got a drinking problem you'll be better off sweating it out on a job. You won't have any time to sit around those damn beer parlors and you might just feel better for it."

And Arne was glad for them and for himself that they lived in a country where the harvest of primary resources still made many opportunities for men with no highly specialized skills and where a willing man could yet climb up a ladder to better pay by diligent hard work.

In each of his postings he would little by little pare the problem down to the last few hard cases whose dependency on handouts was so entrenched that death itself wouldn't scare them into the job market. Then for these he developed jobs on a piece-work basis, jobs they could do for the Agency which were of some use in their communities—cutting wood for the old people, cleaning snow off the school grounds, cleaning out the irrigation ditches. It wasn't efficient but it was useful, and it dealt with the objection that the absolute dead beats still got help while those who tried on their own got nothing.

But no sooner had he found a sense of certainty that he was doing the right, even if damnably unpleasant and difficult, thing about the dependency of the apparently fit and employable than doubts and objections began to raise themselves.

First of all, this hard-nosed approach to the problem was alien to provincial practice, and therefore the Indian people under his administration were not being treated equally with non-Indians applying to provincial welfare offices.

Secondly, the province and Indian Affairs came to an agreement that Indian people resident off the reserves for more than one year would be the responsibility of provincial offices. Therefore there was inequality in the treatment received by Indians according to the place of their residence, since off the reserve they would receive welfare automatically on request.

Arne even found a few instances where men had tired of the demands of the jobs they had found and had simply moved to shacks off the reserve, then obtained assistance from the province.

Arne went to the provincial social work supervisor to find some way his service could be coordinated with that of the province. He explained the policy he had followed and the success he had enjoyed in getting men into employment and the consequent difficulty of the inequalities and the shift of a few off reserve just so they could draw assistance again rather than work.

He knew the arguments, he'd heard them before, but he was taken aback nonetheless.

"Mr. Saunders, I think I have to tell you that you are a most unfortunate anachronism in the field of social work.

"You give no indication of appreciating the psychological needs of your clients. On the contrary, you have been wholly obsessed with meeting your own emotional needs, based on your very Protestant attitude about the virtues of hard work.

"I'm sure *you* feel ever so much better when you force a client to find a job which is clearly distasteful to him. I'm not at all sure your client feels any better.

"It is also clear that your whole approach to social allowance administration is based on your belief that you are protecting the public purse against the demands of your clients. Surely, Mr. Saunders, it would be more appropriate to recognize that your primary obligation is to your client and *his* needs. After all, we are not a poor society. It isn't as if we can't afford a few dollars for people unable to adjust to the rather unrelenting demands of industrialization.

"And surely, Mr. Saunders, of all people the Indian people should receive some sympathy in this regard. We have disrupted their way of life and forced our whole industrial value system on them. If they find it too much, is it really more than we can afford to assure them at least the means to life and a little dignity?

"After all, we aren't even that certain ourselves of the validity of this immense value notion we have about work. By the time you have forced the Indians to accept it, we might well be past its use ourselves. Post industrial society is the question of the day, Saunders, not industrial society.

"Post industrial society will require us to know how to use leisure, not how to tolerate the boredom of industrial employments.

"The guaranteed annual income is just around the corner. Within a generation it is bound to be a fact of life in our society. Men will only work if they feel they want to. Guaranteed income will provide a basis for living, and only those who want something more will be obliged to engage in the little remaining work which will have to be done.

"And, Mr. Saunders, people aren't going to have to have a contest with a government administrator every month for the allowance which is their fundamental right in an affluent society.

"Frankly, Mr. Saunders, I find your whole approach to be negative and, I must say it, fearfully punitive. I am deeply concerned for your clients."

Which was the end of that.

Arne plodded back to his own office and on the way bought

a copy of the Vancouver *Telegram*. It would be delivered to his home and he'd have it that evening but just now he felt as though he had only enough energy left to read a newspaper and, the hell with everything, that's what he proposed to do.

A headline caught his eye at once.

INDIANS SPEAK UP FOR RIGHTS

At the close of a two-day conference in Vancouver today attended by representatives of Indian bands and organizations in the Lower Mainland and Vancouver Island, Bill Jim, outspoken Indian leader from the Fraser Valley said the day had come when white society could no longer get away with closing its doors on Indian people.

"We're demanding our rights," he said in an exclusive interview with a *Telegram* reporter. "The days of inferior education for Indian children on the reserves and no job training opportunities and no jobs is going to be over.

"It's going to be over because if it isn't the white man is going to be sitting on a time bomb and we are that time bomb," he added.

Mr. Jim spoke after the more than twenty delegates had hammered out policy statements on everything ranging from job discrimination to housing and more help for the poor.

The conference was told by Mr. Jim that the rate of unemployment among Indian people was a disgrace to the affluent society and that it was high time the doors of opportunity were flung open to Indian people.

"Our people have a right to the better jobs of society, not just the menial ones the white man thinks are good enough for Indians," Mr. Jim declared in the interview. "We are demanding the right to good job training and good jobs. We are demanding a right to share in the fruits of the abundant society."

Arne folded the paper and shoved it under his arm.

You tell 'em. That a boy. You tell 'em. Go ahead and demand your rights and demand your jobs and demand the fruits and whatever the hell else enters your head.

But, by the Lord Harry, let me tell you one thing and the same goes for all your kids I've tried to persuade to stay in school and go on to job training and all the whole damn bit.

Before you learn anything else, learn how to work. Because if you don't learn how to work, you'll never learn anything else worth a turkey's gobble.

18

The Yucla–Davis Bay Indian Agency embraced the southern portions of the mid section of the mainland coast and the profusion of islands which broke up the mouths of the inlets.

It was a land of steep mountains and dense rain forest, of tide beaches and rivers, of salmon and halibut and cod, of the flooding and ebbing of the ocean into and out of the inlets, of howling southeast gales in winter, of fog in the morning and glorious sunny days on the sea in summer.

It was a land of middens, where discarded shells lay thirty feet deep at the ancestral sites of the people in favored coves and bays near the clam beds.

It was a land now of fishermen and loggers, where hard work paid big money and good salmon years paid big money, and bad salmon years meant big debts on the fisherman's account at the company office.

It was a land of isolation and hard drinking and businessmen and missionaries, of coastal freighters and small boats and logging trucks and steel cable.

It was a land of masks and rattles and totem poles and memories of the long house. It was a land where in living memory men had had the right to kill a slave to demonstrate disdain of wealth.

Arne Saunders brought his family into Yucla to occupy the Agency residence. A comfortable house, it was provided by the Branch since neither renting nor buying in Yucla was feasible for a man subject to transfer at the will of his employer.

Yucla, with its population of fifteen hundred people, hung

on the hillside above the beach at the head of a small inlet; half of it was Indian reserve and the other half, the white end, was an incorporated village municipality.

Unless you had lived there for a while you wouldn't know where the line lay. Some of the Indian people had houses of their own building superior to many in the white end, and the range of affluence was much the same in both groups.

But differences became apparent. The merchant class lived in the white end, most of the seine boat skippers lived on the reserve. Government offices centered in the white end, the long house and the soccer field were focal points on the reserve. There had been for many years a great deal of intermarrying and so the two communities were made one by the blood tie. And some non-Indians lived by choice on the reserve while some Indians lived by choice in the incorporated village. All the children attended one provincial school.

There was prosperity and poverty in both ends.

But while much made Yucla one community, much kept it apart as two. The Indian people clung to a consciousness of their difference and to their grievances against the white man. The land of the province had never been paid for, the services to the reserve were never adequate, the money for new houses was never enough.

The white people objected to the excessive amounts poured into the Indian reserve. The Indians had the same chance on the coast as anyone else. When Indian Affairs installed the sewer system on the reserve, the white end reflected a little bitterly that they would never, themselves, be able to afford such a facility; especially, they said, while their income taxes had to stay so high as to support that kind of a give-away program to others whose economic opportunity was every bit as good as their own.

The Agency residence was located on the reserve and it was run-of-the-mill middle-class housing, better than most on the reserve, though not so good as the best. There was a white picket fence around the yard and when Arne and his family arrived, they scrubbed off the dirty words the white pickets had invited some child to scribble, and set about settling in. Most of the burden of that, of unpacking and putting away and making meals in the middle of it all, fell to Stella and the girls, for Arne had the office to settle into as well. But the girls, Anne and Doreen, were thirteen and eleven now and a fair help, if you pushed them a bit.

Then, rather suddenly, the ingredients of life in Yucla closed in upon them.

Half a dozen Indian children, perhaps six to twelve in age, came into the yard to shout obscenities. Stella went out to ask them to leave and caught a barrage of profanity and foul names that took her breath away.

Half dazed and half angry, she got them out the gate.

The next day the words were back on the fence and when she set again about scrubbing them off, again a pack of children began baiting her with obscenities.

She ignored them. When the words were off the fence she retreated without a backward glance into the house. From there she looked cautiously out of a window. Some children were busy scribbling, others shouting.

In the days that followed children in an age group up to about twelve years virtually declared war on the property.

They tore the rearview mirror from Arne's Land Rover, and shoved mud through the slight opening Stella had left in the window of her small car for ventilation.

They ripped pickets from the fence and on forays into the yard tore up the shrubbery. They threw rocks at Arne's old Labrador dog.

They were incredibly fast of foot and Stella soon realized it would be pointless to chase them in hope of thrashing them because she had no certainty of catching them up, and to give chase and fail would only encourage them to worse deeds. Furthermore, Arne explained to her, she could be taken into court if she so much as laid a hand on one of them.

The girls went to school and at once Anne discovered that while her age group hadn't taken part in the assaults on the property they had other tactics. They challenged her to fight and when she didn't respond—violence was so alien she had no idea how to respond—they gave her lessons in what was expected.

A timid youngster, she could only take the beatings. It infuriated her, but she had no capacity to fight back.

Although Arne and Stella tried on several more occasions to

have the girls walk to school it inevitably ended in Anne taking a beating. So they gave it up and drove the children back and forth the mile to and from the school, through the reserve and into the white end.

Arne had to accept that for his daughters to walk in broad daylight on the streets of Yucla was not safe.

Arne spoke with the RCMP only to find that the sergeant's own youngster was having just the same trouble. For Arne's problems it would be difficult to frame a specific offense out of the highly annoying but very general badgering practised around Arne's house; and assault against a child by a child is so easily defended as ordinary playground squabbling that you could rarely prove it was anything more.

Which only confirmed Arne's conviction that enforcement was no solution, but he had felt a responsibility to his family, especially to Anne, to explore it.

Another element cut into Stella's heart: the calculated and dispassionate cruelty she saw on the street between the children or by the children to animals.

Older children tripped or kicked younger children, viciously, without sometimes even interrupting their conversation with a chum. When the smaller child gathered himself from the ground and, crying piteously, made his way along again, he might not have existed for all anyone paid him the least attention.

Stella tried to give comfort once to such a child only to have the youngster turn firmly away.

Children found crabs under the rocks on the beach and brought them to the pavement where they dropped rocks on them or pulled their legs off to watch, with casual interest, the death struggles.

The dealer at the fuel wharf told of several small boys carrying a puppy out on the wharf and dropping it in the water some distance from shore. While the puppy swam to shore the boys ran back along the wharf. As the puppy came out of the water they grasped it and ran out on the wharf to drop it in again.

The dealer had been busy fueling boats and the significance of what the children were doing was a little slow to sink in. When he realized it and dashed over to stop them they had almost succeeded in killing the puppy by exhaustion and drowning—which they readily admitted was the point of their game.

It was hard in the midst of all this to remember the other side: the warmth and kindness of those people on the reserve who extended their friendship.

One child in particular, Anne's age, became the bright light of welcome in an atmosphere heavy with hostility. She lived nearby. Her father was a fisherman and her mother worked in the laundry at the hospital. They had a large family and aunts and grandparents lived with them, sharing in the care of the children while the mother worked.

Flora was her name and regularly she came with a shy little laugh to visit with Anne and Doreen. Soon Anne and Doreen could visit her house and watch television or read comic books, two entertainments of the age which Arne personally couldn't stand and wouldn't have around.

But fundamentally Flora's family held the same values as the Saunders did. Arne used this fact to explain and make tolerable the predominantly hostile attitude of the others.

"Look, kids, it's a question of values and how kids are brought up and how their parents were brought up.

"Flora's dad and mum care for each other and care for their kids. Their dads and mums cared for them when they were small. They comfort each other when something goes wrong, and because they care for each other, they feel friendly to other people.

"Flora's dad works hard during fishing season and they don't spend all he makes right then, they make it last to buy the things they need through the year. And her mum works hard. They all work hard and help to make their life what they want it to be.

"Now working hard isn't some kind of a virtue all by itself. If you work hard for the wrong things there's nothing to be said for it.

"But working hard to meet your own needs and the needs of each other in the family is good. It means you aren't a burden to others and it's maybe the best way of living your love of the others in your family.

"You notice that when Flora's dad isn't fishing he's usually busy at something else that's useful. He'll be out gathering logs to cut for firewood so they don't have to put out cash for fuel oil. Sure, fuel oil is more convenient but they've decided they can do better by doing the work involved in burning wood.

"Now the dads of some of the kids who seem so mean aren't like that. They catch fish when the runs are on but they spend the money as fast as they make it, a lot of it on liquor. We hear them, noisy on the streets all night after the fishing.

"When the money's gone and the season is over they go on unemployment insurance, but when Flora's dad is hustling wood or out catching some cod to eat, those other people are spending a lot of their time in the beer parlors. And they aren't just spending time. They're spending money that could be better spent on the care of their kids.

"Well, people who are indifferent to the needs of their kids in one way are usually indifferent in other ways too. They don't show them the love and kindness they need and the kids grow up mean and cruel, just the way you see them. You can't blame kids for being hostile if they grow up in homes like that.

"But you see we share values with Flora's people, and this is why we think well of them and they think well of us."

Then more seriously, to Stella: "Still, I think we have to *accept* the people who don't share our values, even if we can't *like* them. I'm just so damn sorry about this racial difference. I fully appreciate why a man might want to sell out and move if several families come into his neighborhood whose values are profoundly different from his own. But if those families happen also to be Indian or Negro or what have you, right away you've got the spectre of rejecting people on racial grounds. Hell, I wouldn't stay in a neighborhood like this for one minute if these were white people acting the same way. What do you make of that?

Stella gave him a thoughtful look. "Oh, I just make you out of that. But you know something else?"

"What?"

"Flora's people won't let her walk from our place to her place alone after dusk. They send her brother over to walk back with her."

It was by talking about their situation in the family gathering that the Saunders tried to keep a perspective on it and help the girls to realize that it was the other youngsters, not themselves, for whom disadvantage was in store in life, irrespective of who was being persecuted at the moment. He explained also that if there were some way they could help those who baited them to change their attitudes, they should do this. "Attitudes are the key to it. If we could change their attitudes toward others we could show them what a lot of happiness people can give each other."

"But there are so many of them and so few of us," Stella countered. "How do you go about it?"

"I don't know. And you get so busy defending your property against the little blighters you forget all your good intentions."

"But I've tried to be nice to them, Arne. Honestly, I have."

"I know. I talked to one of the councillors about it last week. He lives up on the hill and he and his wife have a lovely home they built without any help from the Branch. They have exactly the same problem and no more idea what to do than we have. And *they* know the parents of these kids well enough to approach them, but you know what happens when they do? The parents tell them the kids can play any place they want, including the poor guy's yard, yet. His lawn is ruined and the flowers his wife tried to grow never got started."

Then one day Arne got fed up. It wasn't when Stella was scrubbing "fuck you" off the fence for the umpteenth time, it was when she gave up scrubbing it off and left it there.

He tore down the picket fence and put up tight page wire with two strands of barbed wire on top of it and a padlock on the gate. Try writing dirt on that, you foul little blighters.

Then when a boy of thirteen took a stick to the fence to see how easily it might be sprung, Arne lit after him with a yell. He caught him in a hundred yards and thrashed his backside with the flat of the hand. If it got him landed in court, the hell with it. But it didn't.

A sequel came to the barbed wire on the fence.

A Company of Young Canadians worker had been in Yucla for some time prior to Arne coming here. He seldom came to Arne's office and Arne found no cause to look him up. He knew the chap had worked to strengthen a committee which attempted to give guidance to young people in trouble with the law and that he had started a summer camping project for an earlier age group. Arne gave financial support from his budget for some Indian boys who attended the camp, and he accepted the other's presence in the community as one more hand at a difficult task.

When the CYC worker left the community, he filed a concluding report, and through a man in the regional office who maintained liaison with the CYC, Arne learned of an interesting inclusion therein.

To demonstrate the continuing problem of negative and unresponsive attitudes among the "establishment" in Yucla, the worker had cited the strands of barbed wire strung by the Indian superintendent along the top of his page wire fence.

Arne made a comment. It exploded from him in fact. It was reminiscent of the words on the fence.

19

T his Indian Agency, headquartering in Yucla, was responsible for a number of villages, including Kwatsi in Davis Bay. Its problems were typical of the dilemma of social assistance and branch aid in general.

There was plenty of economic opportunity, there had been for many years and it appeared there would be for many more. It took hard work and inconvenience at times to make use of this opportunity, no mistaking that. But it was there, and no hard-to-come-by sophisticated skills stood between a man and using it.

There were many successful Indian people in terms of the present economy and the life of the coast. These men owned their own seine boats, trollers, or gill-netters, or skippered a seine boat for a fishing company. Many of them logged as well during the closed season on fishing. Some had abandoned fishing due to the unpredictability of its fortunes and now stayed year round in logging.

Fishing had the disadvantage that it came in boom and bust. To make it pay over the long term a man had to make the good years carry the poor ones and to put aside much of the take in the good years for reinvestment in equipment.

It called for hard work, for careful management of money, for denying oneself and one's family luxuries and the status of luxuries when the money was at hand and a choice about its use had to be made.

But men made it pay. By staring out with a rental boat they could work their way up into a better boat. With the first junky gill-netter paid for, turn it in for a better one. That paid for, go for a bigger one yet. Do all your own maintenance in the off season, be raring to go when the sockeye jump, and no big bill to pay at the shipyard.

Hustle and sweat, pay your way, stay off the booze, and you could make it.

There were men with good houses, well-clothed families and debt-free boats as living proof of it.

Then there were those others. They never graduated from the rental gill-net boat. In a big season they lived high, drank the best. In a poor season, they sank into debt. They were forever broke, and since the fishing season lasted only from June through September, the rest of the year was lean pickings, a time to get relief from the Indian agent and dig clams for beer money.

On the principle that you issue assistance when people are in need and not on whether they deserve it, these people qualified much of the time for assistance.

But if you denied assistance because opportunities existed to earn a living, you issued nothing.

And children would undoubtedly go hungry, though there was no assurance that they wouldn't still go hungry even if you issued assistance.

One of Arne's field officers complained to him that he was obliged to issue assistance to a man whose annual earnings exceeded his own. The fellow had got it all at once at the end of fishing and spent it in three weeks.

Arne was finally reconciled, with occasional relapses, to issuing assistance when people were broke, regardless of how much money they had gone through to get that way or of what opportunities they refused to take to earn their own living. He could not go on with what were obviously judged by others in the field of social work to be negative and punitive practices.

And so it happened that in his first dealings with Sammy Joseph, while Sammy was still in Hugger's Inlet, he had resisted like hell giving the man assistance but later relented.

Jobs were scarce at Hugger's Inlet but a small logging operation had begun down the inlet a few miles under contract with the timber company that held the forest management license. It wouldn't last, and it didn't affect Arne's belief that the future for the Hugger's Inlet people lay in getting out, but it meant there were jobs for the time being and, damn it, men should take them.

Most of the men did and finally, after a long struggle, so did Sammy. And to everyone's surprise, though he'd been on assistance since nobody could remember when, he turned out to be a handy enough logger. The job lasted until the operation closed a few weeks before the people moved.

But when they moved, Sammy didn't get started again before the proximity of the beer parlor in David Bay got the better of him and Arne, no longer convinced he was right to insist on a man going to work, put him on assistance.

He would have thought that having given into the dictates of professional social work practice, he at least might have freed himself of the personal turmoil he experienced in the conflict of his own values with those of his clients. Certainly this was how he imagined it had happened at first, and he felt relieved of a nagging burden.

Then one night he had been over to Davis Bay on the thirty-five miles of tortuous road which connected the two communities and though it was after eleven he decided to drive home rather than lodge at the hotel and lie awake listening to the noise of the drinking in the hotel and on the streets.

On his way out where the road wound along above the shore, he saw a light on a wharf. He remembered that the Chief had pointed out to him that the logging contractor who had been a short time in Hugger's Inlet now lived there.

Curious as to what the man might now be doing he stopped the car and found his way down to the wharf. It was a dirty night and under a makeshift tarpaulin shelter a man had the pieces of a motor laid out under the light of an electric extension lamp, the cord of which led back in the darkness to a house above the beach.

The man looked up and Arne spoke.

"Hullo. I'm Saunders. Work for Indian Affairs. I used to see you up Hugger's Inlet when you were logging there."

"Oh yeh. I remember."

"I'm sorry but I've forgotten your name."

"Johnson. Bill Johnson." And he sat back on his heels from his work, letting a large wrench lie loose in his hand. With the wrench he indicated the pieces of motor: "Goddamn starter off'n my boat. Givin' me trouble."

"What do you do these days, since you finished in Hugger's Inlet?" Arne had an honest interest in the activities of men who did the kinds of work that he himself once had done.

"Loggin'. Tryin' to get outa the hole. Lost money in that damn Hugger's Inlet thing."

"What went wrong?"

"See, the only reason I got it to start with, the company knew there was this bit of overmature cedar and a little spruce on a point all by itself. That side of the inlet was logged before but highgraded. When the company got it in their timber license they wouldn't be going back in till it's ready to log the whole thing proper again, so they offered it to contract. There's not much else left for small guys like me, so I tried it. It wasn't worth a damn."

"I'm sorry to hear that. You gave a lot of employment to the people up there for a while."

"They did better than I did."

In the silence that followed the wrench moved idly up and down in the gnarled hand that held it.

Then: "You givin' Sammy Joseph relief now?"

"I'm not really supposed to discuss it."

"Well, you must be."

"Well, yes, I am."

The silence went on and when Johnson broke it again, it was in bitterness and anger. "You goddamn government people, you don't know what you're doing. That guy was turnin' into a good man, if you'd just left him alone. I started on a little job across the inlet here just after those fellas moved in and I did my goddamnedest to get him goin' again. There's nothin' wrong with him once he gets off his chair and away from that bloody bottle. Worst thing about him, he won't take any responsibility for anything. But damn it, he can *work*. He did okay up Hugger's. He made more money there than I did.

"Sure, it's tough work. When we get a wet fall of snow it's a hell of a job but goddamnit, outside of some touch like you got, what the hell *isn't* a tough job around here?

"I'll tell you something else you've never thought about. I pay taxes. Either I'm losing my shirt in some damn bad show or I'm making a few dollars and, bang, I'm paying taxes.

"I'm no big operator and I'll never be one. If I make four, five thousand a year, I'm lucky. I could do better I guess if I'd just go on wages for a big outfit but I try to make it contracting.

"But damn you government bastards, I work hard. When my daughter got married I wanted to give her a good wedding and I went like hell all year and everything looked fine but I figured out my income tax so it wouldn't catch me all at once and it took all the cash I'd saved out of the whole year's work.

"And we're the guys pay the taxes in this country, us working stiffs. It isn't some high paid bastard behind a desk. There aren't enough of 'em. It's us guys that scrape and hustle and never make more'n just enough to get by. We're the guys that carry the country on our backs and don't you forget it.

"And I'm bloody fed up with my money going to feed a bunch of bastard that won't do a goddamn thing for themselves. And it isn't just Indians. There's a bunch of white guys around here the same. They got that social worker convinced there's something wrong with them, they can't get jobs.

"Godamnit, *anybody* can get a job in this country. The logging outfits are flying guys in from Vancouver steady. All you gotta do is show up for work every day and tough it out.

"So I go over there every day and tough it out on that sidehill in the mud and the rain and you take some of my hard work and give it to Sammy Joseph so he doesn't have to go out and tough it out with me.

"You think that's fair? I wouldn't mind if it was somebody else paying the taxes but it's guys like me just barely getting by that's paying for it all."

Saunders broke in: "I think I read a statistic to that effect once, I'm sure you're right."

"Sure I'm right. So what the hell are you doing? You're putting that whole bunch at Kwatsi on relief and I'm paying for it."

"I'm sorry it seems that way."

"I'm sorry too. Now I gotta fix this motor. It'll take me half the night and I have to get it back in the boat to get to work in the morning."

Arne left him to his struggle for a living—with some left over to pay taxes so Sammy wouldn't have to struggle.

But, Lord, it's not so simple, for I would take Bill Johnson's struggle any day to Sammy's.

But Bill Johnson cannot see it that way and I cannot offer him any valid reason why he should.

There must be simpler jobs than being an Indian agent.

20

Hugger's Inlet reached like a long arm of desolation into the steep mountains of the coastal backbone, forming a deepening trough sixty miles in length. Fog rolled into the trough in summer and rain in solid sheets obliterated it in winter. Occasional days of pure sunshine exposed in it such exceptional splendor as to make only more dismal the unrelenting dullness of its normal condition.

But here the salmon had come in their spawning runs and here the clams had proliferated on the beaches, and so here too had come a handful of those people of tide beach and salmon river who have populated this coast for longer than anyone knows.

And for many centuries they lived a life of which much has been said but perhaps little is known.

The sea, the beach and the river fed them. As essential as anything else about their technology was the knowledge of where and when to wait for nature to disgorge her abundance: to deliver her salmon, her shellfish, her halibut, her oolichan, and the edible growths on her tide-swept shores.

The forest housed and clothed them, and the same rains that grew the forests rotted away the evidence of their living as soon as in their living they discarded an object or abandoned a dwelling place.

As with all people, out of the associations between each other essential to the survival of the race, their society evolved its ways and, as with all people, there was more or less of joy and sadness, love and cruelty, sureness and anxiety.

There were art forms and mystical dances, there were wars and slavery, there was courage and cowardice.

There was a way of living and it worked. In its terms, some succeeded and others did not. It has been ever thus with people.

But by the sixth decade of the twentieth century, more had changed in a hundred and fifty years than had changed in all likelihood in as many centuries before that.

The Indian people of Hugger's Inlet whose ancestors had lived by the sea and the tide beach and the river and the forest now lived also by the cannery and the fish boat, the power saw and the log landing, the clam buyer and the bootlegger, the post office and the storekeeper.

And money. Green paper and silver coins. Money. Glittering excitements in the cannery store. Money. Many numbers in a little book in the company office. Pop and potato chips. Money. Owe money. Get paid money. Credit. Debt. Liquor. Puke on the board walk in front of the cannery shacks in the cold of the dawn. How much for a new motor? Clothes for the kids. There's no money. The manager says we have no money. But what happened to all them fish we delivered?

See Joe. Borrow some money. Joe makes lots of money, he's got big seine boat, all his and paid for.

Money.

Yes, there had been changes to life as it had been lived by the Hugger's Inlet people.

Arne Saunders could not find a beginning and unravel it all.

He could only take stock of what he found, measure it by the functional yardsticks of the nineteen-sixties and pursue results hopefully useful in all the directions of his accountability—to the people, to his conscience, to the Branch, to the instant (or not so instant) experts who damned all the failures of his program, whose right to damn he had never questioned.

On taking charge of the Agency he found somewhat fewer than two hundred Indian people living in this isolated village in badly run-down housing without running water.

A cannery that used to provide shore work was closed, logging operations which had been frequent in the vicinity were now scarce and the store at Last Harbour had shut. Although the fishing companies still competed to buy fish, the run-down rental boats and the few privately owned boats in the community couldn't weather even some parts of the inlet during the stiff afternoon westerlies of the best part of the fishing season, let alone the trek across the open to Davis Bay for supplies.

Operating a day school was a nightmare.

Teachers wouldn't go to live any longer where they could not enjoy city-quality services. In fact, the more isolated the location, the more convenient the services must be. Not only must there be a power plant, but it must be adequate to run an automatic oil furnace, refrigerator, electric iron, toaster, record player and hair dryer although nobody but a school teacher, Arne profoundly suspected, would ever need to use all her appliances at precisely the same time every day.

And would know less about running a power plant.

But even when the building was there and the pressurized water system functioned, when the fuel had been barged in and the tradesmen had been flown in and out for the endless maintenance problems so far beyond the experience of anyone in the village as to be hopeless for them to attempt, even then the problem wasn't solved.

For without detracting a jot from the inestimable service given to Indian youngsters by some dedicated teachers Arne had known, he had long since faced the reality that there weren't enough of those to go around and the kind who reached Hugger's Inlet most years couldn't have found teaching jobs against any competition.

There was no competition for Hugger's Inlet.

Then for the rare youngster who graduated from the semblance of elementary school taught there, going on meant residential school or boarding out in the lower mainland. Either meant such an environmental upheaval that only three youngsters in the whole village had ever endured it for more than one additional grade. And apart from the question of education, there was something profoundly disquieting in the provision of spacious living quarters, running water, a flush toilet, a complete range of electrical appliances, modern furniture, and a cost of living bonus to a succession of privileged outsiders, few of whom, if any, could be seen by the people of Hugger's Inlet to do anything tangible for the future of their children.

With the best will in the world, no man in Hugger's Inlet could ever earn enough money to enable his family to live like that.

Yet without all that, nobody would come to teach.

The magic wand of government, of which in Arne's developing experience all people expected all things, would not perform the necessary miracle in this matter of schooling at Hugger's Inlet.

Nor would it perform anything in housing and services for the people themselves without untenable anomalies resulting.

If it made sense to expect any modest participation in industrial life by the people of Hugger's Inlet, it made none to invest public funds in housing where there was a scarcity of employment and the very spending of money on necessities for life meant putting life at risk in small boats on an angry sea.

Still, did any government administrator have the wisdom or the right to influence profoundly—and there are few influences so profound as the dispensation of shelter—where people might live?

There was a subsidy program in housing for Indian people by which a limited but sound house could be built for a family in Hugger's Inlet, covering virtually the total cost.

Was it for Arne to say they should not have it in Hugger's Inlet? To predict that Hugger's Inlet had no future then help the fulfillment of the prediction by withholding the means by which it might be prevented from coming to pass?

Hugger's Inlet, for all the gloom of its winter rains, was home to a people to whom home was essentially a matter of place—this beach, this river, the sight of that mountain across the inlet.

North American industrial man has tampered so fiercely with his roots that he imagines he can transport them in moving vans with his household effects so that he may scramble on the ladder of organizational promotion. But not the people of Hugger's Inlet.

It was Sammy Joseph who put words to it in the only assertive utterance Arne ever heard from him: "He's our home town this old place. You give us little relief, we get by. We go someplace else, we not belong that place. Even we got reserve like you say down Davis Bay, that only place where some people used to camp for clams when they makin' reserve in old days. Our old people, he's all buried this place."

But what was the good of a little relief when there was no store left to spend it in, short of a trip across the open in those damn gill-net boats, even supposing you could believe that life could be lived on a little relief?

And what about the children and the grandchildren? For all the hazards of how they lived, their population was growing rapidly. Where this generation needed twenty-five houses, the next would need fifty, the one after that a hundred or more. Whatever Arne foresaw doing, if it was done in Hugger's Inlet it meant putting props under something that could never stand on its own and, having the props, it would grow and grow, and as it grew it would need more props. Once the precedent was set, it would get more props and go on growing.

There was one man who believed absolutely that the people must move to Davis Bay. Billy Williams, the old elected chief, was obsessed with this one idea that moving out would save the people.

In most respects, he was realistic.

He did not drink and in this he was one of very few.

He knew that good jobs were hard to come by and that somehow people had to live in terms of present realities.

He knew that his people drank too much and lived too violently for their own well-being.

He knew that it made no sense to build new houses in Hugger's Inlet.

He knew that the availability of liquor in Davis Bay would be ruinous to most of the adults and many of the teen-agers.

He knew that Indian Affairs could never find the kind of teacher year after year who could prepare the children in Hugger's Inlet for the world outside it.

He knew that too many boats had set out in too many storms never to be seen again, that too many children had died unattended by a doctor when the weather hadn't permitted setting out at all.

Arne Saunders listened to the old man's dream: the people must move to Davis Bay to the Kwatsi Reserve and it will be hard for the adults, many of them will never be any good again. But it is all on account of the children. They will go to school with the white children and have the same good teachers. They'll understand all the things they don't understand now, that none of the people understand. They will learn what they need to live a good life.

It won't be like it is now when they go out after they've only been to school in Hugger's Inlet Indian day school and come back by Christmas all angry and silent and not giving a damn about anything but drinking.

They'll get in those good schools right at the start and they'll make a whole new life in the next generation because they'll have as good a chance as the white kids.

And Arne, anxious for support for his own beliefs about the futility of Hugger's Inlet, believed everything the old man said about how bad it was in Hugger's Inlet.

He hadn't the heart to tell him what a pipe dream it was to believe in the efficacy of the schools when it came to making a whole new life in one generation.

21

The people did not easily agree. They feared the unknowns of living in a strange place. They had been to Davis Bay to shop and to drink and some had tied up there during parts of the fishing season. But Davis Bay lay outside the homelands of Hugger's Inlet people.

Arne and Billy Williams supported each other, reinforcing their conviction that they were right, contrary to the doubts and fears of the people. They held meetings and Arne explained that the Branch would build houses and install water and eventually indoor toilets hooked to a sewer system. It would take time, it wouldn't happen all at once. But even if the Branch built houses at Hugger's Inlet, there wasn't enough money to build for everyone at once.

There would be jobs for the men. The big companies in the forest operations at Davis Bay were flying men in from Vancouver all the time and they were glad to hire local people instead.

And schooling. The Chief mostly talked about the schooling. Arne feared he was laying that part on a bit too thick, but he didn't know how to stop him.

There were a few questions.

"You gonna give us little relief, Mr. Saunders, if we havin' a hard time by Davis Bay? We not too sure. People don't know us there."

"There'll always be assistance if you really need it. But you know you shouldn't get assistance wherever you are if there's work."

"If we stay here, you gonna give us little relief? No jobs here now."

"I just don't see how you can make a good life on relief. I think your only chance is to move to where there's work and the other things you need as well—stores, school, doctor and so on."

But finally there seemed to be acceptance of the inevitable. No one liked the idea of moving but Arne felt he'd convinced them that to stay was a dead end.

He worked out a plan with the Chief and the councillors.

The Agency would build the first ten houses at Davis Bay and install the first stage of the water system next year. Then the first families could move in time to have their children in school in September.

This would mean that there would be an insufficient number of children to keep the school going at Hugger's Inlet, so the parents still there would let their children go to the residential school until more houses were completed.

Over about four years the housing could be completed and even if there were still some crowding, it couldn't be any worse than the way they were crowded into these shacks and worn-out houses in the old village.

Arne explained that the regional office was very interested in the move and had assured him of as much money as possible each year until the new village was well underway. But of course there were urgent needs everywhere in the region and no band could have all its needs met in one year.

So finally the work began. The land on the Kwatsi Reserve was cleared, roads built, a water system installed and ten houses built. The money available had been stretched to build the ten houses and in most of them there was a little work left, but it was of such a simple sort that Arne felt sure the people themselves could manage.

Late that summer the people moved, not just the ten families but the whole group. They came in their boats with everything they could pack on board and by the time Arne knew of it, it had all taken place.

They crowded into the houses, sometimes three families to a house, until the houses could hold no more. The rest tied their gillnetters in the river or at the float a mile away in front of Davis Bay and lived on board.

No one ever lived again in Hugger's Inlet.

22

I t was hell.

Even in the shacks and run-down houses in Hugger's Inlet the accommodation problem had never been so acute. People hadn't had to spend the winter on a gill-net boat or share with not just one but two other families in a house.

It may have been the case (indeed it was the case), that for more than a generation the people had not set any impressive standard for themselves in housing: nonetheless they had managed to maintain a semblance of a separate dwelling place for each family.

On the boats, in the crowded houses and in the bars in Davis Bay the drinking went out of control like a runaway forest fire and nothing could stop it. The few couples who had come to grips with drinking at some time in the past saved themselves because they knew the danger, but they could not save the others, not even their own young sons and daughters.

With their few resources pouring into liquor, the people had little for essentials. The children, walking a mile along a path exposed to the southeast gales in insufficient clothing, came soaked to school.

Everybody fell sick with colds and flu.

The outhouse holes filled with rain water and one family installing a septic tank found the water table so close to the surface that the drain field from the tank barely functioned. The people resorted to buckets which they carried to the sea each day, while Arne renewed his request for funds to install a sewer system.

But money is not in endless supply. With the whole group moving at once, do you install a sewage system for these ten houses or do you extend the water system and build more houses first?

Since the funds were limited even in emergencies—Arne knew that most of what Indian Affairs faced in the entire B.C. Yukon Region was an emergency of one kind or another—you set priorities.

The priorities were duly set: first build more houses and a water system and go on packing sewage to the sea, unless the people want to try outhouses on the higher ground where there is enough drainage so the holes won't fill with water. But they'll have to decide that for themselves.

The way they were drinking, they wouldn't be deciding anything for themselves. Not for a long, long time.

Why in hell did they all move at once?

Because, Billy explained in his halting way, the first to get houses were the ones everyone else leaned on for boat trips across the strait, for borrowing supplies between trips, for decisions in the community, for the fundamental assurance that a man could survive.

Some are weak and some are strong and the weak cannot stay behind when the strong move on.

Then why in hell didn't someone tell me?

Because nobody knew, it just turned out that way.

Which Arne accepted. He just wondered why he had been stupid enough not to foresee it himself.

23

T he next year Arne had built six more houses and the year after that three, and an extension to the water system.

He had had eleven other bands, none with any particular sympathy for the Hugger's Inlet people, making insistent demands for solutions to two families in one house situations in their villages as well.

Then the next year three and finally, in the year of the death in her crib of Sammy Joseph's baby, in 1969, there were four more to be built, and while housing in Kwatsi would still not be abundant, it would be on a standard as good as any in the Agency, save in some communities where heads of families over many years had invested heavily from their fishing income in houses of their own building.

In 1967 Indian Affairs hired a community development worker for Kwatsi in recognition that whether the government has limited or unlimited funds, the government cannot do for Kwatsi those things which Kwatsi must do for itself and without which all that the government might do cannot mean anything in the long term.

The appointment came with others throughout Canada, following on a realization that existing programs in housing and physical development, in education and training and in direct physical support, were not breaking the pattern of failure in Indian communities.

The worker was to function in a catalytic role.

He was to discover leadership, not become a leader himself.

He was to foster leadership, but not hold its hand and thereby disable it.

He was to inspire people to identify their own crucial problems, not point them out himself.

He was to stimulate people to find their own solutions, not introduce the solutions himself.

He was to start people talking to each other again when they had stopped, stir their courage when they had given up, rebuild their faith in themselves when it had broken down.

Arne welcomed the appointment but in Kwatsi he had little hope.

He was surprised.

The worker was a man of thirty, a little unsettled, a product of four years at university, an arts degree, and several employments of which he had tired or grown disillusioned. He had taught briefly in an Indian school, been a social worker for a short while, had sold insurance and given it up; and yet for all this apparent indecision had something solid and resourceful about him.

Carl Brothers was his name and soon he was just Carl to everybody and Arne wondered why, since he never consciously wanted the people to do otherwise, they never called him Arne. It was always Mr. Saunders, except for a few who had succeeded in life very much in the way Arne saw success, and when these used his first name he felt the warmth of their acceptance. And yet he was sure he didn't normally imply the need for formality. He knew his position had a fearful lot of authority wrapped up in it but he tried to exercise it in directly level ways, even when he felt the need for blunt talk and firmness. But Carl was Carl and he was Mr. Saunders.

Well, no matter, the point was he got along well with Carl. So, obviously, did the people and, by golly, something came of Carl's being there.

The council began to meet more often and committees formed up to solve some local problems.

A bus was hired to take the children to school and paid for from a collection made in the village.

The bus was a success but eventually the collections couldn't be maintained. But the committee was able to argue that attendance had improved, that dry kids did better than wet ones, and that though the distance was less than normally called for a bus it was warrantable for Indian Affairs to support it financially.

The committee members persuaded Arne, who in turn supported their petition to the officer in Region who controlled the education budget.

Another committee tackled the neglect of children during drinking bouts. In meetings with the provincial social worker a scheme developed in which the committee made placements for emergency care which the worker ratified after the event with his statutory authority. Indian Affairs met the actual expenses.

The outstanding achievement was the pre-kindergarten. The people obtained an old float house from a logging company and hauled it ashore. They salvaged lumber from a building being demolished in Davis Bay with which they restored the float house, refinishing the interior and rebuilding the roof. When the job was done not one man in the village had failed to put in some volunteer time. Then a committee formed to put the little school—*my* school the little ones called it—into operation, and by obtaining grants from both provincial and federal sources they were able to hire a teacher from Davis Bay and pay one of their own women as an aide.

The principal in Davis Bay said the improvement in readiness for the school program of the children coming from the pre-kindergarten was nothing less than striking.

Arne wasn't blind to the fact that most of the people's initiatives resulted in a demand on public funds to meet the cost of what they were doing but surely this was a fair price for initiative where none, it seemed, had been before.

And what about Carl? Clearly, none of these actions would have been taken without him: clearly also, though he dropped starters here and there, he didn't do all the fire tending. It was the members of committee or council who came to Arne and they did their own talking, talking based on having thought something through.

Oh, the village still suffered all its ills. The drinking continued, maybe even got worse. Men weren't going out looking for jobs and social assistance was climbing. Children were still neglected and filth in dirty houses wasn't any less.

And not everything turned out happily. Many times something useful might have been done but for disagreement as to what to do, for failure of someone to perform, for want of determination.

But surely, Arne believed, it is better that these few things have happened than that nothing happened.

Carl threw new light on Arne's action in the community. In the hotel one evening after a council meeting he said bluntly: "You're not involving the people in the things you're doing for them."

Arne checked a defensive impulse. How could anyone be more involved than to be the sole beneficiaries of this whole investment in roads and water system and housing? "I don't understand."

"You're doing it for them but you're not doing it with them."

Carl gave him time to think and Arne's mind went back to the meetings in Hugger's Inlet. He explained about the meetings, and then how he'd worked out the plans with the council to relocate the people.

"That was fine as far as it went. But after that, what happened?"

"Well, hell, we got on with the job. We put in the roads and the water and got the first ten houses up."

"Who decided where the roads should go and where the water intake should be? Who planned the house sites?"

"The engineering staff from Regional office. Who else? These kind of questions have to be settled on engineering considerations. Remember, this is a hell of a tough site and we have very limited funds. The whole design is dictated by what's the least costly way to get the most serviced house lots."

"I understand that. You understand that. Do the people understand that?"

"Well, I guess they do. At least I've taken it for granted they did." Then after a moment of doubt: "Okay, I'm ready to learn something. You tell me what it is you want me to figure out for myself."

"I think you've just figured it out. Or you've started."

"Tell me anyway. It's faster."

"There's part of your problem. Too efficient. You always have to find the shortest, fastest way to an end product. Trouble with people is their lives consist of going places, not with arriving. So the going has to have the quality in it.

"But back on this other thing, I'll tell you if you like and mainly it's not a difference in objectives but in how we ought to reach them.

"You haven't shown enough faith in the people. Just because their lives are messed up with personal failure doesn't mean they can't focus on a problem and a set of facts and make a judgment.

"The best place for them to try is in a community problem, not a personal problem. It's still vital to them but just far enough removed that their experience of personal failure won't lick them before they start.

"So maybe it would have been a good idea if as many of the adults as possible could have met here on the site with the engineer before any planning was done just to talk about the physical problems.

"The plan would have been the same in the end and the engineer would have taken all the site data and done all the drawing, the same as it's actually happened.

"But the people would have had a stake in it. The engineer's plan would have been their plan too.

"Same thing with the houses. How many of the people chose the plan for their house?"

Arne had a slightly trapped feeling. "There wasn't any choosing, damn it. How could there be? We needed as many three bedroom houses as we could possibly produce with the money we had. You get into minimum cost public housing and choice goes out the window. You standardize across the board to pare costs to the bone. If people want a choice in housing they have to put a devil of a lot more of their own money into it than these people do."

"Okay, let's accept that. But don't you think the people in Kwatsi could have accepted that too?"

"I think so."

"But you never discussed it with them from the premise of the physical problems you faced."

"No. I didn't."

"Do you know why you didn't?"

"Because I never really thought about it. I've just realized that now. And maybe I lacked faith in their ability to deal with problems. They don't have an impressive success record."

"Maybe. Anyway, all I'm saying is that what you're doing is by and large all anyone could do under the circumstances except that you've missed the importance of letting them share the problems with you. All the problems. Right now they're not sure you know what you're doing."

"That a fact?"

"That's a fact."

"Well, I'll be damned."

So Arne went to the next council meeting with all his budget data and a stack of plans and engineering reports. He laid all the facts on the table, literally, and for three hours he stifled his impatience while the little group of uncertain people wrestled with too many needs and not enough money, too many families and not enough houses, too much ground water and not enough slope.

In the end they agreed what should be done with the limited funds in Arne's budget.

It was precisely what he'd had in mind himself.

And this freshness of view which Carl brought to the work was encouraging; still, Arne could not dislodge the hopelessness he felt about Kwatsi.

The burden of leadership fell on too few shoulders. The same sad and burdened people served on all the committees, wrote up all the petitions, attended all the meetings.

But whole rows of houses remained with doors shut to community action. These same houses took in much liquor and spilled forth much drunkenness, much violence and many ragged children, while a mound of filth and broken windows gathered around and in them.

A man cast his wife from his bed and took his oldest daughter. One day he forced his wife and all the other children to go out in the street in the rain and forbade them to return. The woman, forced at last to seek help, went to Carl. But she wanted only to be allowed back in the house with the children. She did not seek recourse for the incest. She wished to lay no charges, give no evidence, only to occupy the house, for she had to have shelter with the other children.

Carl went to the house and the man in a rage drove him away. Carl saw the girl in the bed, but by itself that proved nothing. The man had been clothed when he opened the door.

Arne shut from his mind the times over fifteen years he had been through that same course: he heard rumor of incest, he investigated, he found a woman in fear of her husband unwilling to give evidence.

Finally the man let his wife back in the house.

The day Arne heard the girl was pregnant he had very little hope for Kwatsi. She was just turned fifteen.

And on balance Arne could not decide whether in the long run this kind of work, this catalytic attempt, described but not defined by the term "community development," could really make an enduring difference against such enormous odds. In any case, after two years and just before the death of Annette Joseph, Carl Brothers was transferred to another posting in a different agency.

24

It was not many days after Corporal Thompson had been to see Arne for some information about Sammy Joseph's social assistance income that he was in Yucla again and dropped by for a different reason.

"Can you bear a little adverse publicity?" he asked. "I think you might get some."

"Why is that?"

"You know Sprague. Davis Bay *Gazette*. He was in. Word got around I've charged Sammy and Eliza. He was pretty mild on it himself. He thinks enough to realize there are no pat solutions and we aren't all just a lot of clods for failing to pull one out of the hat. But he says he thinks the Vancouver papers might pick it up and do a standard 'pity the poor Indian held down by the dirty government' kind of story. They can't focus on the charge against Sammy too much. It's in front of the court. But they can have a deal on Kwatsi. He just thinks it's likely. They haven't had one for a while, and Sprague says it's routine."

Arne shrugged and spun a paper clip on a small clear space on his desk top. It went out of orbit and landed on the floor. "No panic. Happens every little while."

"You're used to a bit of criticism."

Arne had a wry feeling and the grin that went with it. "You might say that. In neon letters a foot high. Several times."

"What do you really feel about it? The constant sniping, I mean."

Arne thought for a while. The question had been seriously put to him and there were no short answers. He didn't want to half answer it, and he took some moments for a rapid sorting of ideas. Thompson waited.

Then: "I think the first point is that everyone, absolutely everyone, has the right to criticize. I'm very conscious of that. It's not just freedom of the press and so forth. What we do for Indians, or *about* Indians, is anyone's legitimate concern.

"Actually, the press bothers me least of all. They're usually off base a mile but nothing I could ever say would persuade them or anyone of it, and since I don't have to give an answer to a newspaper, it's simple. I just heave it aside.

"But I have a strong feeling, probably totally unreasonable, that I ought to make a convincing response to direct criticism. It almost has the effect of making me accountable to any idiot with a bone to pick.

"And of course it's impossible because most of what we do is a damned if you do and damned if you don't kind of thing.

"You issue social assistance and you're sapping people's initiative. You don't, and you're being punitive and imposing your own values on them.

"You build houses and you're paternalistic. You don't and why the hell haven't you for God's sake, look at this mess.

"You stretch your budget as far as you can and try to build a basic house for as many people as possible and some guy says how do you expect shacks like that to hold up? Would *you* live in one yourself? But if you go a little extra on each one and maybe build a few less, you're squandering the taxpayers' cash.

"And, you know, we do have to try to be proficient at a

staggering variety of jobs. If I'm spending a lot of time trying to be fair in a social assistance program and make a mistake somewhere on a drainage problem, the roof falls in. Every practical man in town tracks me down to tell me what an ass I am.

"If we don't supervise our local contractors they cheat us left and right. Chisel the government is fair game. Then the same guys spend the rest of the winter belittling us for the money we wasted on the job. If we supervise enough to prevent it, we're overloaded with high-priced help.

"And the Indian people do the same thing. The council persuades us to give somebody some new roofing. They really need it and you can count on it they'll put it to good use. Well they don't, you know. They damn near never do. But that same council never lets us forget how we wasted that roofing and why don't we do something with all that money that'll do some good.

"In no village have we as much program money as the village wants or could put to good use. But *every* village rants at me that the reason they're short is I've got favorites somewhere else. I've spent hours explaining the yardsticks I've used to be fair about it, but they're not interested in that part.

"But the hardest criticism to take is maybe the hardest to explain, and maybe I'm hypersensitive to the fact that in almost everything I do and especially in social work, I'm an amateur at a professional game.

"It seems as though for every hard fact of my experience there's a piece of sophisticated theory that denies what I see with my own eyes. And some guy with a degree looking down his nose to make sure I hear about it.

"But before I go into that, one thing I should make clear: social scientists generally agree there's no difference between ethnic groups in potential ability carried in the gene pool. There are no superior or inferior races. I think someone tried to put a dent in that recently, something about the exceptional incidence of genius in certain directions in the Jewish gene pool. There was all kinds of alarm, talk about harking back to Hitler and his master race crap.

"Well, I'm sure as hell not competent to argue that point although I think the reaction to the proposition was as much as anything emotional and based on our intense commitment to the grand egalitarian ideal. I don't see why in the long course of evolution one gene pool shouldn't come out ahead of another in qualities that provide ability to succeed in certain kinds of situations or environments.

"Maybe the problem Indian people suffer is that the kind of ability their evolution produced for them isn't useful in the new situation. I could find it reasonable that the kind of inherent ability refined by natural selection for use in a direct relationship with the primal environment would not be the same as one evolved in a heavy overlayer of technology. And we've had a heavy overlayer of technology in our environment for thousands of years.

"If that is the case, then our attempt to make industrial man out of Indians and Eskimos, which is far from a howling success you know, may have more injustice in it than subsidizing them enough to let them go on with the fragments of their old life. Although I think that's impossible, so I really didn't say much there.

"But my point was that I have no argument to make one way or the other on the proposition that all ethnic groups are born equal, as it were.

"But I do claim it as a fact of present realities that a seriously large number of Indian people in most Indian communities don't have the ability to manage. Whether they were born without the potential or whether they were born with it and failed to benefit from it because of the destructiveness of their surroundings does not alter the reality that here and now they don't have it. Not all, but a seriously large number in most communities.

"And there's a line up of professional opinion that says, in effect, this isn't true. I can give you some typical positions.

" 'Indians don't do as well in the fishing industry as others, not because they don't manage the job well enough on their own part, but because the white man won't extend them any credit for capital investment in equipment.

" 'Indians are just as capable as anyone else of handling money and credit. The only reason they can't get credit is the stereotype the white man has of the Indian.

" 'Poverty among Indians is just an economic problem. Provide economic assistance on a generous basis and there won't be any more poverty.

" 'The reason Indian people don't succeed as well as others in managing their communities is that the white man has never let them.'

"I could go on. But maybe the best illustration is something that happened at the management seminar we had in Vancouver last year. Every so often a group of superintendents is gathered up for three weeks of workshop sessions and we get discussion leaders from the university and consulting firms and what have you. It's pretty useful, makes you think.

"Well, this guy from the university decided to cut through some of our biases. He passed around a questionnaire designed to make people of any level of management make a qualitative judgment about the competence of people several levels down from them and a couple of levels above.

"Evidently the results are always the same. Every level of management thinks the levels above them have about the same competence as they do, but that the levels below are decidedly inferior in ability to make operating decisions, manage large financial budgets and so on.

"In our case the levels below were our own staffs followed then by the band councils and the band membership.

"I smelled a rat and refused to complete the form. But everybody else went along and did an honest job of it. The results showed the inevitable: that the superintendents as a group thought the band councils and the band membership had less of the cross section of management skills than they possessed themselves.

"Well, you should have seen the guy perform. He had the whole roomful squirming with guilt for the next twenty minutes. What a bunch of prejudiced bastards *they* were. And, of all people, a group of Indian Affairs employees. What a disappointment.

"But all those guys had been guilty of was honesty about the reality of their own experience. I don't claim to be the epitome of success in the management of my personal resources, but I can tell you without a shadow of doubt that if on average in any Indian village on this coast the management of personal resources was as good as my own, there'd be little deficiency in physical plant or standard of living.

"But that fact out of my direct experience is written off as a myth growing out of my own psychological need to fortify my self-image by stereotyping Indians as an inferior group.

"Take the question of credit. I'll give you two instances.

"There's a village up on the Tunahan River in the interior and there were two small grocery stores when I was there, each about a mile from the village in different directions. Both extended thirty-day credit to three or four people in the village who had demonstrated they could handle it. Both stores extended thirty-day credit to all but a few of the non-Indians in the district.

"Gather statistics on a situation like that and you can draw a prime picture of discrimination. Ninety per cent of the whites get credit while only 10 per cent of the Indians have the same opportunity. No wonder the Indians fail, getting treated like that.

"Well, one of the stores sold out and the new owner came in determined to be fair to the Indians. She extended thirty-day credit to anyone with any regular source of income. Within three months she was on the verge of bankruptcy and her life's savings were out in credit in that village. She cut her losses just in time. And when she went back to strictly cash they still spent enough that it was clear they'd had the resources to use the credit. But they lacked something else essential to the use of credit that most of the non-Indians in the district obviously had.

"Other instance relates to the liquor problem as well. A couple I know have a store at Sound Bay. They've been in business there for over twenty years. They deal with loggers and fishermen, many of them Indian and many of them not.

"Before Indian people had unrestricted access to liquor, whether a man was white or Indian had nothing to do with his getting credit. Credit was available to everyone in the district except a few who had been unfair about it.

"Then came liquor and one by one the Indian people lost their ability to use credit. Now there are a small handful still able to use it but to protect their own finances the couple running the store has had to refuse it to the majority.

"But to come out clean on that questionnaire, I'd have had to have said of those people that they possessed, currently, as much functional skill for management as I do.

"I don't think that guy from the university had ever worked in an Indian community and I got nowhere trying to explain why I thought what he was doing wasn't valid.

"Now I know that the man who generalizes from experience runs the risk of generalizing from too limited experience. But can you write off as myth what his experience tells him just because it runs counter to a piece of social theory?

"That's what bothers me most, I guess. And I get a real anxiety up whenever I want to tell it how I find it, for fear I'm going to be labelled prejudiced and guilty of unfounded notions about racial differences."

Arne set the fourth paper clip into a practised spin and watched it lose its momentum. Thompson meanwhile retrieved the three which had spun off on the floor at his feet while Arne had been talking. "You must cost the taxpayer a lot of paper clips in the course of a year."

"Yeh," Arne said, slowly. "Best thing I do." Then on subject again: "You know, I'm getting cranky when people tackle me about something I've done or failed to do. I'm going to have to do something about it.

"You know Joe Simmy? Lives around the village from house to house. No place of his own. We built him a place on the reserve at the mouth of Chout Creek. He'd asked to have it there. About four years ago. But he was hardly ever in the place. He'd be away for days at a time, and one time some kids got in and wrecked his stuff and damaged the house pretty badly. He never went back and now there's nothing left. He could have straightened it up if he'd got at it right away but I guess he didn't have the heart.

"Well, now he's got about the worst accommodation problem in the village. He's been borrowing a corner to sleep in here and there till everybody's fed up with him, and we just haven't had the funds to build him another place. The council won't give him any priority for another subsidy. He hasn't done anything about it himself, but then I guess you couldn't expect him to.

"So he stopped me the other day and he was half looped up and did he ever go after my hide about what the hell kind of an Indian agent was I anyway?

"Something snapped. I lost my temper and I chewed that poor guy out from hell to breakfast. What the devil was he doing for himself anyway besides shovelling all his problems off onto me? Why, damnit, hadn't he looked after the first house he got? Didn't he have enough guts to drag himself away from that beer parlor? What the hell kind of a man was he, anyway?

"Well, it was pretty fearful, and did I ever feel badly afterward.

"Then some truck driver in Davis Bay made a comment about were we going to go on building houses for these people forever, and maybe he wished his skin was dark too so he could get a free house.

"Wherewith I tore a chunk off him. Didn't he have enough brains in his head to appreciate the bind these people were in? Couldn't he see we had to help them over the hump till they could get their feet on the ground again? He never got another but in edgewise.

"I'm getting edgy. I'm an uncivil civil servant."

Thompson got up to go. "Understandable I guess. But you know what blew you off at Joe Simmy is the same thing that made me lay this charge. There must be a point where you hold a man responsible. Who *else* are you going to hold responsible for things so immediately the result of what a man does?"

"Well," Arne offered, "the theory is that people caught up in these self-destructive behavior patterns aren't there by choice. Classic example, at the end of the fishing season a lot of these guys get a settlement from the company that would see them through the winter in absolute comfort. Grub and clothes for the kids and a few new things for the house. It's no pipe dream, I've seen the accounts. Some of them play it just that way and really get ahead. But take the guy who blows her all in a week. He and his family suffer, and I really mean *suffer*, all winter long. Oh, we issue him some assistance but the way he lives, it doesn't help much. And don't ever think he'd try to make that money last if we didn't issue assistance after he's blown it. I've tried that. Given guys notice and stuck to my guns. Makes no difference.

"So who *do* you hold responsible? If that guy was responsible he wouldn't be like that. People who see the situation from the outside, they're distressed by his poverty, they hold the government responsible. We ruined him, we made him that way. We ought to change him, they figure. But nobody really knows how to change him. We sure as hell don't, and those guys in the university don't know either. They have a lot of classy theories about it but I haven't seen one of them come out here yet where the action is and do anything."

25

The news item in the Davis Bay *Gazette* was unflavored.

POLICE CHARGE PARENTS IN CHILD DEATH

The RCMP have laid a charge against the parents of an eleven-month old girl following her death in Kwatsi village on June twenty-sixth.

The charge, under a little used section of the Criminal Code, alleges that the parents dealt with the child in a manner that was likely to leave the child exposed to risk without protection.

Arne read it and he thought a long time about Sammy Joseph. Which led him to think a long time about Arne Saunders.

But thinking did not tell him who might have prevented the death of Annette, nor how.

26

Sarah hated the school and she wasn't going back after the summer even if she wouldn't be sixteen until nearly Christmas. Anyway she didn't pass grade six, and what good was it to go back?

She only liked school once. When she was in grade one she

had Miss Markin and Miss Markin let her do things in school she liked. That was after the first teacher in grade one. She didn't remember, but she thought she must have been two years in grade one. Miss Markin let her make pictures.

When she came to Davis Bay all the kids walked from the village and the white kids called them dirty Indians. She kicked a white girl and got in trouble. The white girl had pinched her nose and made a face when Sarah sat in the seat in the next row. The teacher had told her to sit there. It was after when she kicked the white kid, but the white kid told.

Sarah didn't have any socks that time. They walked in the mud by the road and the bottoms came off her shoes. Some of the kids had rubbers.

Sarah watched for her mother to come back up the middle of the village. When she got back, Sarah would get out of the house. Her mother had told her to mind the baby when she left. She'd gone down to the Willies' to see if she could get a drink, probably. Maybe the Willies would have some wine.

Finally Sarah left anyway because she got tired of waiting. The baby wasn't crying and Tommy could give her a bottle if she woke up. There was some milk in the bottle on the table from this morning. She told Tommy before she left. He said a bunch of dirty things but she didn't stop to hit him. She should have.

Anyway Winnifred should have been back. She'd gone with her baby to town and left Nola and Terry. Sarah didn't like Nola. She was always fooling around. Anything Sarah wanted to do, Nola was fooling around all the time.

Sarah went over to her friend's house, Louisa Fred's. She liked to go there because she and Louisa could close the door and be alone in one of the rooms. Louisa had some magazines and Sarah got so she could read the stories. They talked lots too. Mostly they talked about being married. Louisa was hoping she and Joe Charlie were going to get married but she didn't know because Joe had been gone over to Yucla quite a while now. But he used to come around her all the time when he was in Kwatsi. Once Louisa talked about Joe and her doing it right there in that same bed where they were talking but after that she never talked about it again. Louisa was a year older than Sarah. Sarah wanted to talk about it but Louisa didn't mention it after that one time.

When Sarah got to Louisa's, Louisa was out so Sarah got one of the magazines and took it home. It was the one had the story in it she liked best. She'd read it enough now it was easy to read and it felt like it was all happening to her. She didn't understand it all because it was about white people but the girl got with this man she loved in the end, and he was good to her because he really fell in love with her. Sarah wondered if Joe had fallen in love with Louisa, if that was what it meant, what Louisa told her about that day because it had sounded different than the time Pete Simmy had caught Sarah by the creek. It was kind of rough the way Pete had done it, like he was mad at her, and it hurt so much she cried after.

Her mother wasn't back yet and Sarah sat on the bed in the room where the baby was. It was where her mother and father slept and Sam Junior too, but he slept on some stuff on the floor because it wasn't a very big bed.

The baby was still quiet and before she started to read Sarah got the bottle and pushed it in her mouth, but she wouldn't suck. She needed her diaper changed but the old lady could change it.

After Sarah started reading, Nola came and began fooling around on the bed. Sarah told her to quit, and after a while she slapped her head because she kept on fooling around.

Winnifred came back and Nola was still crying and Winnifred got mad about it. She never even asked if Sarah'd hit her. Any time Nola cried it was Sarah's fault. But Winnifred got tired of Nola crying and slapped her herself and sent her outside.

Winnifred asked where the old lady was and Sarah said she didn't know. Winnifred sounded like she'd had a little to drink but not much. Winnifred didn't drink much.

She had some store bread and stuff she'd got from town. She'd have got it off the relief. The relief went to the store and it was hard to get the stuff because half the time the storekeeper said they'd already got all was coming and they couldn't draw ahead.

Her dad said most probably the Indian agent and the storekeeper were taking some of it, that was why it was short all the time.

Sarah took some of the bread and went back into the room with the baby to eat it while she read. She took it while Winnifred was in her room, and when Winnifred came out Isaac and Norma were taking some too, and she slapped them away from it. They came in where Sarah was, and she saw they still had the bread they'd taken. Winnifred said why couldn't they wait, grabbing stuff all the time.

The old lady came back and she was a little drunk and she got a little noisy for a while. She didn't get noisy very much when Sammy was around, so she made up for it other times.

She shouted at Winnifred for a while in their own language and Sarah didn't get much of it because ever since she was in the school at Hugger's Inlet she got so mixed up between the different words she never got it straight again. Now the kids were all talking white and old people got mad because the kids only could understand some of their own language but they couldn't talk it. Sarah could understand the old lady except when the old lady got drunk she couldn't make out half of it.

Pretty soon the old lady came in and lay on the bed so Sarah left the room. The baby was still quiet. You could smell the wine the old lady had been drinking.

Her dad came home and it was still in the afternoon. He had a half gallon of wine and he'd had some of it already. Sarah went to Louisa's again but Louisa still wasn't around. But Sarah stayed in her room for a while anyway and read some more in a magazine.

When she got home again later her dad was drinking the wine and Jimmy Joseph was there too. He was drinking some of the wine. Winnifred was having some too and the old lady was in the kitchen but she wasn't drinking. She was pretty sleepy.

After a while Jimmy left and Winnifred went to her room. Her dad finished the wine and went in and lay on his bed. The bread was on the table open so Sarah took some and ate it with some fish that was left from the day before. The other kids came and got some then and Sarah watched the old lady, but she didn't seem to notice.

Later on Winnifred came out of her room again and fixed some milk, one bottle for her own baby and one for Annette. She told the old lady she was fixing milk and the old lady went in by the crib but she didn't do anything, she just stood there, and when Winnifred brought one of the bottles the old lady tried to give it to the baby, but the baby wouldn't take it. She had a cold and her nose was runny.

Sarah watched for a while because she was wondering why the baby wouldn't take any milk. She hadn't taken any milk all day. But when she saw the old lady wasn't going to change the baby, Sarah went to her own room so the old lady couldn't tell her to do it.

She still had the magazine so she read the story again, the part at the end. Isaac and Norma were in the room for a while but she told them to quit fooling around and they went outside.

It was still light but after she finished reading the story she closed her eyes and just lay on the bed. She thought about Louisa and Joe and tried to remember exactly what Louisa had said that one time she told Sarah about her and Joe in Louisa's room. She'd got excited just by Louisa telling it and she tried to get the same feeling again by remembering it. She'd watched her dad and the old lady when they were drunk and they'd do it right in front of the kids, but that just made her ashamed. She couldn't get the feeling from that.

After it got dark she went outside and down to the beach. She'd been holding on for quite a while till it got dark because the bucket was full and she didn't want to have to pack it out. Isaac or Tommy should have packed it out but they'd go outside anytime, even in the daytime just in the bushes a short way and leave the bucket. Sometimes Sarah had to pack it out if she couldn't wait till it got dark. The little ones would use it at night even if it was full and when the handle got spilled on Sarah hated to pick it up to pack it out.

She went back to the house right away and soon Isaac and Norma came in. They all went into the room where the three of them slept, Sarah and Norma in one bed and Isaac in the other, and got on the beds to go to sleep. Sarah made Isaac take his shoes off, but Norma wasn't wearing any.

Sarah was restless and soon she made Norma go over to Isaac's bed. Isaac would fool around with her if he was awake but Sarah made sure he was asleep first, before she made Norma move to the other bed.

It was real dark when the two white guys came to the door. Sarah answered the door and asked what they wanted and they walked in and said they were just visiting.

Winnifred came out of her room and one of the white guys, the big one, said to the other this'll sure do and then Sarah's dad came in the room.

The guys said they just wanted to visit and they had some beer and wine and they put some of it on the floor and on the table and opened some bottles and passed them around. Sarah took one of the bottles of beer and sat away from everybody else a little. Sometimes she could drink some beer and nobody'd say anything but sometimes Winnifred would get real mad and slap her around. This time Winnifred never said anything, she just drank the beer and some of the wine and talked to the white guys.

Sarah just drank the one bottle and got feeling a little high just on the one bottle but the others drank quite a lot and pretty soon they were all pretty drunk, especially her dad and the old lady.

Finally one of the white guys, the big one, said to the other he figured it was about time and then he came over to where she was and gave her some more beer and asked her what her name was. She told him and he said he sure liked her a lot and he wanted to talk to her alone. She got kind of scared but she said they could go into her room and he brought some wine left in a bottle with him when they went in her room. Before he took the one bottle he gave another one to her dad but her dad was too drunk to hold it so he put it on the floor beside him. Winnifred and the other white guy were still drinking on the bed where Tommy slept in the front room but Winnifred had sent Tommy in to sleep in her own room already.

The big white guy pulled her down on the bed right away and she got scared and stiffened up. He stopped and asked her what was the matter, didn't she want it, and she said she was scared.

He told her not to be scared, he wasn't going to hurt her and he got her to drink a little of the wine. It burned in her stomach and made her feel warm and he began to talk gently to her and this time he didn't grab her, he just began to feel her with his hands. After a while he told her he loved her, even though he hadn't seen her before, but he'd been watching her all evening and he knew she was the girl he wanted.

She didn't feel so scared any more and she knew he was going to do it to her and she began to feel excited the way she had when Louisa had told about her and Joe.

Still it was quite a while before he did it and then it never hurt, only afterward she felt kind of empty. It wasn't what she expected and the excitement left her suddenly about halfway through, and she had a feeling it was stupid what they were doing.

But she slept afterward and then he woke her up to do it again later and it was all right, only this time he didn't say anything or tell her he loved her or anything like that. In the middle of it one of the kids got up to use the bucket and you could hear it spilling over and it seemed to make him mad for a minute.

She had to go after that and she went outside. After she came in she went to look at the baby.

Right away she knew something was really wrong with the baby. She touched the baby and the baby seemed different, and she pulled her hand back and tried to wake the old lady and then her dad but they were both passed right out.

Winnifred and the other white guy were on the bed in the front room and she shook Winnifred but she couldn't wake her up and then she didn't know what to do so she went back in her room and told the white guy something was awful wrong with the baby.

He got up and came with her to the crib and put his hand on the baby and then said there wasn't anything she could do, just go back to bed and tell her mother in the morning. Then he went out and shook the other guy awake, real rough and told him c'mon, we got to get the hell out of here, and they left.

Sarah drank the last of the wine in the bottle in her room and fell asleep even though she was scared about the baby. When Winnifred told her the next morning the baby was dead she never said anything about looking at her in the night.

27

Lucky and Bruce were real old buddies. Anything worth doing, they did her and they did her together too.

They were a couple of real top high ball fallers. Boy, they could lay the tall trees down like damn near nobody else.

They could lay a few other things, too, any chance they got. And they made big money. Any contract they couldn't make a thousand dollars a month on apiece, hell she wasn't good enough for a pair of real high ball fallers like Lucky and Bruce.

They made her hard so they spent her hard. Boy, they'd drunk their way from one end of this old loggin' show to the other, every place worth drinkin' in from Vancouver to Prince Rupert. And laid a squaw in every Indian town besides.

"Hey, Bruce. Lookit this in the local rag. About this kid dyin' an' the old man gets took up for it."

Bruce lounged on his bed in the bunk house cubicle he shared with Lucky, contemplating the socks on his propped up feet. They were getting gummy and he'd have to change them.

"Whose kid an' whose old man?"

"By God, that's that same place we was in that night at Kwatsi. I told ya that kid was dead. Boy, I had a hell of a time wakin' you up to get outa there fast enough."

Bruce thought about that. "Yah. Well I was sure some corned up. I never even made it into that bitch. But you got that young one, huh?"

"Damn right. Old Lucky never gets so drunk he can't score. But by God I had to soften her up some. She started out like a chunka left over fish. Said she was scared. But I told her I loved her, she was the gal I been waitin' for all my life. Boy, that's the line to give 'em. Pretty soon she wanted it so bad she could hardly wait."

"Way to go, boy."

"Took her twice too. Only one a them goddamn kids got up to use that stinkin' crap bucket right in the middle of it an' damn near made me sick."

"Can't win 'em all."

"Can't win em all. But I sure get my share. Damn, but your feet stink. When you gonna change them socks?"

28

T he Vancouver *Telegram* was a hard-hitting newspaper, and Matt Delaire intended to keep it that way. As though its impetus began in the very staccato of his voice, he issued loud instructions predicated to bring the news stories rolling home to the pages of the *Telegram* in the shape Matt Delaire wanted them.

He sent for Art Ladner, as likely a man as any to do the job he had presently in mind.

"What can I do for you, Matt?"

"Go up the coast to Davis Bay. There's an Indian village there, Kwatsi. Bunch of people the Indian Department moved in from some Godforsaken place up one a' the inlets. Picked up an item here. Kid died and the local cop charged the parents. Some obscure section in the Code. Can't touch that, of course. But I want a good solid story on how the Department treats those Indians. It isn't the kid's parents going to be responsible for that kid, it's the Department. Know what I mean?"

"Got you."

"You'll have to be careful about the charge against the parents. Just mention it in passing. But make the message clear. Okay?"

"Will do."

"Take Phil Robinson with you for pictures. You can concentrate on your pencil."

"Right."

29

Art made enough inquiries to find out which house the kid had died in, but they couldn't stand the stink in that one so they moved along a couple of doors. This one would do. Lots of clutter for the photos, but not so smelly you couldn't stomach it.

He explained to the woman that they were from the newspaper in Vancouver. "We'd like to take some pictures and talk to you a little. It won't take long."

They got inside and Art thought at first the woman was going to get hostile but it turned out she was just confused and a little drunk. He tried to explain again but he couldn't make out whether she knew what he was talking about or not.

So he took charge of what he wanted to do for a few shots of the place and when she went along with it he breathed easy. Hurdle over.

"Look, Phil, there's no story here unless we get this crowded up a bit." Everyone in the house was in the one room but it didn't have the cramming it would need for impact in the picture. "Go round up a few kids outside while I get some names."

Phil came back with half a dozen curious youngsters and he staged the whole thing along one wall where a stove and makeshift sink already helped give a crammed appearance.

He made half a dozen exposures with a few variations. "That ought to do. Now I'll just cruise around the village for some outside stuff, Art, while you pick up some copy."

Art couldn't get anything from the people in the house. He went out and stopped two men walking down the middle of the village.

"Hi. I wonder if I could ask you a few questions. I'm from the newspaper in Vancouver, the *Telegram*. I understand you fellas have a pretty hard time here. What about this Indian agent? Is he pretty tough to get along with?"

It was about all the opener he could think of and for a while nothing happened. Like the woman in the house, these guys didn't seem to have much response and Art began to wonder if they understood enough English.

A few more people came up and Art repeated his pitch. Slowly one or two began to talk and then the whole thing grew on its own.

"You're pretty crowded here. You don't have many houses."

"Yeh. We had houses up Hugger's. But the Indian agent, he movin' us here. He supposed to build everybody new house but he don't build half a them. Just only a few."

Soon he didn't need the leading questions.

"We had good life up Hugger's. Lots of Indian food, you know. And jobs. We got jobs up Hugger's. No jobs here."

"No sewer here. S'posed to be sewer. An' we only got three four outhouse for whole village. Don't know why he won't do nothin' about them outhouses."

"We had our own school up Hugger's. It was good school."

"Hard time to make a livin' sellin' clams. He don't give us much relief, you know."

Art had difficulty keeping up. It was as though the people seldom had a chance to tell their grief to anyone and once they started, it poured out. Many joined the group and all began giving information without even asking who he was. Some of them were drinking, quite a number actually, but they all had something to say when they saw he was interested in the way the Indian Department had treated them.

Some of them spoke as though he knew things about their village or their private lives already, and that confused him a bit. He never did figure that out, except that he became more convinced than ever that they hadn't any real idea who he was. And some of the things they told him were a little hard to tie down in specifics. Like the little school shack. It was some sort of kindergarten they ran themselves or perhaps with the help of someone called Carl. In any case, the Indian Department hadn't provided it, that was clear.

But he could fill that in later from someone else. He'd got about all he needed here. He joined Phil at the taxi they had kept standing by and returned to the hotel in Davis Bay.

From the hotel Art telephoned the Indian Affairs office at Yucla and asked a few questions just to be sure he didn't goof on some of the things the Indians had alleged. Mainly he wanted to know about the kindergarten. That sounds a little too complicated to handle without verified facts.

Conveniently, he was able to put the Indian Affairs man, Saunders, at ease over the phone. He was a little guarded to start with but he explained readily about the kindergarten. Indian Affairs hadn't helped with the building, the people had done that on their own, though the Department helped now with a grant toward operating costs.

But for the most part Art really didn't need another version. It was good copy, damn good copy, just the way they'd told it themselves at the village.

He relaxed with a drink in the hotel room with Phil and in his mind began putting the story together. With the pictures it would make a good page.

30

It made good copy. Indeed, Arne Saunders read it with considerable interest when it appeared in the weekend edition of the *Telegram*.

INDIANS DISENCHANTED BY FORCED MOVE

Davis Bay, August 7

Over two hundred Indian people crowded into twenty-two box-like houses on the Kwatsi Reserve near this upcoast community have profound misgivings today about their Indian Department sponsored relocation, four years after they were moved from their ancestral homesite in remote Hugger's Inlet.

Men and women crowded around a reporter-photographer team from the *Telegram* who visited the reserve today and poured out a story of broken promises and hardship following on the move the Indian agent persuaded them to make, ostensibly for better housing, schooling and employment opportunities.

Only ten houses were found to be ready when the group arrived, notwithstanding promises made during meetings in Hugger's Inlet that a new village would be provided, complete with running water and sewer. Four years later there are still only twenty-two houses and no sewage disposal system.

HAD A GOOD LIFE IN HUGGER'S INLET

Informants told of a frugal but adequate life in Hugger's Inlet.

With occasional employment in scattered logging camps and abundant sources of their traditional food in the salmon rivers and clam beaches they lived a secure though isolated life.

Indian Affairs had built a school on their reserve with modern accommodation for the teacher and informants expressed puzzlement as to why schooling was one of the inducements used to persuade them to leave.

Indian Affairs issued social assistance to offset unemployment from time to time but never to the extent made necessary by the dislocation in their way of life created by the move, according to one spokesman.

FORCED TO MOVE

But the threat that assistance would be withheld was a major factor in forcing the people to agree to the move.

"We had no choice," this spokesman said. "The Indian agent told us we wouldn't get any relief or any help with new houses as long as we stayed in Hugger's."

Indian Affairs also closed the day school as soon as the first ten houses had been built at Kwatsi, seventy miles away across the open strait.

LIVED ON GILL-NET BOATS

Unable to crowd into houses already occupied by two and three families to a house, others spent the first winter in small gill-net boats tied up in the river at the village or a mile away at the government float in Davis Bay.

Indian Affairs did not at first provide a school bus and

children walking in the rain to and from school had no place to dry clothing in the crowded houses and small boats.

Informants said there had never been so much sickness and some children have died of pneumonia each winter since the move.

SEWAGE CARRIED IN BUCKETS TO THE SEA

With no sewer system nor any indoor plumbing, the disposal of sewage has been and remains a major problem.

Some families use makeshift outhouses while most use a bucket indoors which they carry out to empty on the beach, creating a line of drenched waste and refuse along the front of the village exposed at every low tide.

DEPARTMENT DIDN'T HELP WITH PRE-KINDERGARTEN

Through their own effort the people have salvaged a discarded float shack previously used by a logging company and turned it into a pre-kindergarten.

"The kids had too hard a time in school," one informant explained. "We had to give them a start."

The school is run by a committee who receive per capita grants to pay a teacher who comes each day from Davis Bay.

"But the Department never helped us with the building. It's sure not much of a building but it's all we could manage because the Department never helped," the informant added.

SOCIAL ASSISTANCE HELD BACK

Other informants complained that the Indian agent has deliberately held back social assistance when people desperately needed it to tide them over the difficulties of adjusting to the new life.

They allege that the jobs the agent said they would be able to get near Davis Bay haven't materialized and they often are reduced to digging clams to eat and to sell to the clam buyers who come from Vancouver during the large tides in the winter.

Signs of apathy are everywhere in the village, in the unkept houses and broken windows, in the broken down cars and litter of the yards.

The people readily admit that drinking is much worse than before. Many of the people who openly spoke of their problems made no effort to hide the fact they had been drinking.

Many children were seen in the village to be poorly clothed. Many were barefoot and none wore coats though the breeze coming in from the sea was chilly.

Some smaller children wore tattered shirts but no pants or diapers.

PARENTS CHARGED IN DEATH

One eleven-month-old child died in her crib recently in one of the houses.

The RCMP have laid a charge against the parents under a little-used section of the Criminal Code which alleges that the parents exposed the child to risk.

There were photographs taking up the rest of the page. Arne gave them a wincing glance and turned to the editorials. He soon found the one he knew would be there: "Once more the officials of the Indian Department have demonstrated their mindless insensitivity to the plight of the people they are paid by the taxpayers of this country to help.

"In story and photographs elsewhere in this issue, the *Telegram* attempts to convey something of the despair which the bungling ineptitude of officialdom has brought into the lives of a band of Indians forcibly moved from their traditional home for what appears to be nothing more than administrative convenience.

"No doubt the Indian Department will have an elaborate justification for what it has perpetrated here; perhaps it will parade unemployment statistics or the cost of extending services to people in the surroundings of their own choosing.

"But nothing the Department can say will justify the human misery behind the facts uncovered in the visit by a *Telegram* reporter and photographer to the Kwatsi Reserve near Davis Bay this week.

"No doubt also the Indian Department can argue that life for these people was no bed of roses in Hugger's Inlet where they came from, and that all the social ills of Kwatsi cannot therefore be blamed on the Department.

"Well, let the Indian Department so argue. But the citizens of this country are not blind to the fact that it has been the paternalism and hand-out practices of this same Department that has reduced these people, long before this last calamitous blunder, to debilitation and dependence.

"The least these same officials might do now is a comprehensive job in housing and municipal services. But even that seems beyond them, as families carry their buckets of sewage to the sea."

And Arne suffered the damnable agony of hindsight. If only he had foreseen that they all would move at once, if only he had had enough money in one budget year to do everything, if only he hadn't thought it reasonable that the people themselves might have taken the trouble to put enough outhouses on the higher ground where they could have been made to work notwithstanding the inconvenience.

If only. Yes. If only. Damn.

31

The woman from the *Herald* arrived in Arne's office the Monday immediately following. She was short and slight and neat and she almost glared through her dark-rimmed glasses. Curtly, she explained that she'd been to Kwatsi and, frankly, she didn't think the *Telegram* had done half the job they could have.

"For one thing, why aren't these people in decent housing right in Davis Bay? If they had to be moved why go on with the reserve nonsense? Surely that was the golden opportunity to make the real change?" The jabbing dark rims punctuated the questions which were really not questions at all but judgments.

Arne replied with caution: "It's a good point. We do have a program through which people with some regular income can buy houses off reserve and it's scaled to income so that anyone could handle it from a financial point of view.

"But mainly it's a question of how people feel about it, and in any discussions I've had with them, they didn't favor breaking up their community to disperse among whites."

She was unimpressed. "I spoke to the women. They don't like having to walk back and forth to town for everything they want. There's no bus service. They're spending a fortune on taxis. Why couldn't you have just got lots in Davis Bay and build the houses there instead? You'd have had them on sewer and piped water and you'd have had to build decent houses instead of those shacks."

"I admit what you say sounds terribly logical. But if people aren't ready for such a big leap into the middle-class city subdivision, is it fair to force it on them? They do have that choice through the off-reserve housing program. But it may be a lot more important right now to hang onto their own community, such as it is, rather than plunge by individual families into something as demanding as Davis Bay could be.

"Can you imagine how they'd be treated over their yards? They have no tradition about growing and cutting lawns and neat little fences. Would they have the freedom to have their yards as dirty and untidy as they presently keep them if they were obliged to live in Davis Bay?"

Again, she was unimpressed. "That's a feeble excuse if every I heard one. What about the sewer? Why hasn't the Department given those people a sewer system?"

"Money."

"What do you mean, money?"

"Just that. We don't have a bottomless barrel of money. We do what we can with what we get. Houses seemed more important until the crowding could be reduced. I know it's tough without a sewer, but I also know one hell of a lot of people in this country solved their own waste problems long before we all got the idea it was the responsibility of the government to do it for us."

She flashed back. "Are you saying the government *shouldn't* give those people a sewer system?"

"No. Just that they might do more of a provisional nature on their own until money becomes available."

"Like what?"

"There is some ground where outhouses will work."

"Who in Canada now uses an outhouse? How primitive do you want people to be? Do *you* use an outhouse?"

"No. But I didn't suffer when I did use one."

She was sharp, no mistaking that. She went back a step and nailed Arne again. "You said some ground. What about where outhouses wouldn't work?"

"Septic tanks with outfalls to the river or the sea. I know that's a pollution problem but a septic tank is pretty fair primary treatment and it would be tolerable until we can build the sewer."

"And *what* would they do for money?"

"They aren't entirely broke. As a matter of fact we bought a tank for one man who insisted he'd install it. It's still lying in his yard."

"So it's all *their* fault."

"I didn't say that. I just said they could have done a little more on their own until we could channel enough money in to install the sewer."

"I think that's the stupidest excuse of all. Do you really think this country can't afford it? Indian Affairs should put running water and full bathroom plumbing into every Indian home everywhere in Canada right now. Not next year or the year after, but *right now*."

Arne decided it was his turn. "Everywhere?" A slight pause.

"Everywhere."

"In the north too? I know some people there who leave their houses frequently in winter to go trapping. Indoor plumbing could be more trouble than it's worth."

"What do you mean?"

"Well, the plumbing would freeze up. Toilets don't drain. They crack if you don't remember to fill them with oil. Then you have to drain all your pipes."

"They'd just have to learn, that's all."

"And in the meantime, what do we do about all the broken plumbing?"

"Fix it! And keep on fixing it until they learn."

"Oh. Well, I guess that doesn't apply in Kwatsi anyway."

Angrily, she changed the subject. "What about this policeman in Davis Bay?"

"Well *what* about him?"

"What kind of an insensitive brute *is* he?"

"I'm sorry. You really have me there. As far as I know he's done his best to deal fairly with the people of Kwatsi."

"Fair? And lay criminal charges against parents who've suffered the loss of a child on top of everything else? Oh God, I could cry when I think of that damn policeman. Strutting around in his oh-so-clean uniform and his polished shiny boots. What does he know of the misery they suffer?"

"Look, I'm afraid I'm not in a position to discuss that."

"Oh no. Of *course* not." The sarcasm cut at him. "You couldn't discuss anything so nitty gritty as *that*. Oh, you can talk about people having dirty yards and frozen water pipes but you can't talk about a damn policeman's inhuman attitudes to the people you're supposed to be here to help."

Arne didn't attempt to reply and in the silence he saw that she was, if nothing else, profoundly distressed by what she believed to be a terrible injustice.

When she began again she was back on the houses. "If you're going to build houses on the reserves instead of in the same communities where everybody else lives, why for heaven's sake don't you build *decent* houses? Those places at Kwatsi are falling apart. It's no wonder they don't look after them. They're just shacks to start with."

"Have you got fifteen minutes?"

"For what?"

"Short trip to the reserve. Right here in Yucla."

"Okay."

The house Arne took her to was small and neatly set in a carefully tended yard.

The woman who let them in was slight and plain and wore a dress from which the color had long ago been washed. She smiled shyly and Arne explained he wanted to show her house to his visitor.

A collection of small children gathered in the room and kept a silence which suggested that a lot of boisterous noise was being suppressed with difficulty.

"Can we look through the house?"

Shyly she nodded and led the way.

There wasn't anything to it. Simple furnishings were crammed in everywhere and in the kitchen a washing machine and tub took up as much room as the stove.

But it had about it the warmth and cleanliness of a much-loved home. For all that was jammed into it, a comfortable tidiness persisted.

After they left Arne waited for the reaction. He had no intention of inviting it.

Finally: "So what was that all about?"

Silently: can't you guess, you idiot? But aloud: "Was that an adequate house? I don't mean splendid or spacious or costly or ambitious. But was it adequate?"

"Sure. It was adequate. As a matter of fact, it was quite pleasant. She could use a bit more room. Did they build it themselves?"

"No. Indian Affairs house. They put in a contribution of exactly one hundred dollars, which is about what most of the people in Kwatsi put in. But for God's sake, get this part. That is exactly the same house we built in Kwatsi except that it's five years older. Same plan, same materials, same limited budget and that family is as crowded as most in Kwatsi. A damn sight more crowded than many whose places are a shambles."

"So?"

"So doesn't that tell you anything?"

"No. Not a thing. Should it?"

"Forget it."

Arne never did read the piece in the *Herald*. But he heard it was a dilly.

32

T he inevitable outrage and indignation followed the publicity. Irate citizens, comfortable in suburbia, wrote scathing letters to the editor. Opposition Members asked questions in the House and the director's office in Ottawa telephoned Arne to get an explanation, *any* kind of explanation, for his having said Indians should be free to keep dirty yards if they want to.

Arne waited with the patience he had learned to be his only defense for the hubbub to die down. Fortuitously, a long summer of labor unrest and strikes, a pending provincial election and an obscenity charge against a hippie newspaper in Vancouver took precedence in the press and public conscience and let Arne off lightly. Without this competition, the horrors of Kwatsi might have held the spotlight for as long as two weeks.

Arne next saw Corporal Thompson when he called at the detachment office in Davis Bay to verify that legal aid had been provided for the defense. It had, which he'd expected, but Thompson was despondent, which he hadn't.

"You sound less than enthusiastic. Bad press get you down a little? That was *me* they were after, you know."

Thompson rotated back and forth, thoughtfully, in his swivel chair then tilted it back to put his feet on his desk. "Oh, fooey on the press. No, I've just got into a bit of a personal bind over this thing and I can't get it sorted out."

"Tell Uncle Arne. Everyone else does. Somebody upstairs pulling the ladder out from under you?"

"Oh no. Nothing like that. The Force doesn't do that to a guy. No, just my own confusion."

"So how? You sound like an Indian agent I know."

"Okay. I'll tell you. I wish I hadn't laid the charge."

Arne shrugged. "So? I hate to tell you how many decisions I regret after I've made 'em. All part of the job."

"Not quite the same as this. See, in police work you lay a charge or you don't lay a charge on the evidence or lack of it that an offense has been committed. You just *don't* let yourself get into the question of whether the guy could help himself or not. If that's anybody's problem it's the judge's problem."

"So, you're worried the evidence isn't adequate to support the charge?"

"No. It is kind of tenuous, but that doesn't bother me. If we lose on that count that's just the way it falls. No, I guess for once I can't get away from the fact that whether you like it or not a policeman makes a judgment every time he decides to lay a charge, and most times it's as cut and dried as you like—but this time it isn't."

"You bothered that maybe Sammy or his wife have lost control, if they ever had it, and that therefore you can't really hold them responsible? That it?"

"One way of putting it. I keep going back to where Sammy started out. Of course I don't know anything in particular about his individual history but I know if you're part of a situation like Kwatsi and Hugger's Inlet, you sure as hell didn't make yourself what you are." Then in afterthought: "If any of us made ourselves what we are."

"Well, you can always go around that circle about free will being a delusion. But we need law enforcement, even if it is just a way of adding to the circumstances which, taken altogether, influence how people act. My doubts begin when the enforcement results only in punishment without any hope of changing how people act."

"Like right now in the case of Sammy Joseph?"

"Yes. Okay. But why should you wrestle with that?"

"Why don't I just hide behind the old evidential argument? Here's the body, Judge, here's the dirty crib, here's the doctor's statement, here's Sammy Joseph who didn't do a damn thing about it, Judge. I'm just the policeman, Judge, so I don't know anything about guilt or innocence. I just gather and present evidence, Judge. I'm clean. You get dirty if you want to, Judge, but I'm clean."

"Now wait a damn minute, Thompson!" Arne interjected. "You're getting awfully close to the raw. You aren't God, and you can't thrash yourself because what looked right one day looks wrong the next."

"Can't I? I'm going to tell you something else. When I laid

that charge I was fed up to here. I was so damn mad I could spit. I'd been trying to help old Billy with those bloody white bastards that go in there with booze looking for women and I couldn't do anything. There was always somebody happy to have them in with their liquor and that killed the trespass section. But Billy couldn't see that, and I was just one more white man who didn't give a damn for an Indian. Then I got in that stinking house of Sammy's and saw how that kid died and I just lost any cool I had left. Whether I should have laid that charge or not I sure as hell shouldn't have laid it in anger."

"What are you going to do now? Can you back out?"

"There's a way to back out. But it requires a very logical presentation of cool facts for the consideration of the attorney general's office. How the devil do I make that kind of submission out of the grindings of my fickle conscience?"

"You sure you belong in police work?"

"Not a bit."

Then Arne said thoughtfully, "I'm sorry I said that the way I did. I'm sure you do belong in police work. But I'm sure for the same reasons it isn't easy. We're all people, you know, and we've got to live with our own weakness as well as tolerate the weakness of others. I just wish I could do a better job of remembering that."

"Yes. Well, I'll find a way out of this one, I guess."

"Let me know, won't you?"

"Sure thing."

33

Quandary cornered Arne.

Joe Bradley, his field officer responsible for several small and moderately isolated villages to the south of Yucla, came to him for guidance.

"It's about these septic tanks in Sound Inlet."

"So?"

"I can't get anyone interested in installing the damn things. They're just lying there on the ground big as life. Right where we dropped them off the barge a year ago."

Arne shrugged. "Maybe nobody's really interested in septic tanks and indoor plumbing."

"Maybe not. But it's kind of late to tell me that. The council insisted this was what they wanted to do with the repair money last year. They decided on six households they figured could handle the installation themselves. Of course, we've been stung on this before so I went around with the Chief to every house and spelled it out very clearly: we'd deliver the tanks and the toilets and the pipe and fittings. *They'd* dig the holes and the trenches, and we'd send in a plumber to help with the fitting. We asked them to think about it and let us know, and we stressed the part about it being self help. If you don't want to do the digging, tell us. We'll go to someone else who does.

"They were really enthusiastic. Fact is, they started giving me a hard time because the stuff wasn't on the next barge. Really a hard time. One or two got downright nasty about it. I explained as best I could."

Arne knew Bradley well. He was a mild-looking man and as mild as he looked. He wouldn't fight back if the whole village ganged up on him. Not scared, just gentle. No fight in him. "So?"

"So the stuff came in finally: tanks, drain pipe, the lot. We staked everything out on the ground for each house so nobody'd be stuck about where to put the tank and lay the field. We made a sketch to show them how deep. And that was the end of it."

"What about the Chief?"

"He says we better hire someone to dig the holes and trenches."

"Like who?"

"Anybody from the village who wants the job, I guess. Maybe the guys themselves."

"The hell with that."

"What should I do?"

"I don't know."

Bradley looked down at his hands and there was despair in his manner. Arne felt sorry for him but it didn't help. "What would you *like* to do?"

Bradley didn't look up. "Get the darn septic tanks installed, I guess."

"Okay. There's two choices. You can pay someone to do the digging and we're just the same old patsy we've always been, and Sound Inlet Indians will be just a little bit lesser people after you're done.

"Or you can take the damn tanks and stuff out of there on the next barge and tell them they obviously didn't need them badly enough to make it worth the taxpayer's while. Except don't say that last bit. But after you take the tanks out the old wheel will keep turning around and sooner or later some newspaper reporter or politician will discover how underprivileged they are, and we'll be right back in there installing septic tanks, if not a full-blown sewer system."

"Which should I do, Arne?"

"I don't know."

"You have to tell me something, Arne. I can't just leave it the way it is."

"Why not? I never thought of that. It's the obvious answer."

Bradley searched Arne's face. "You mean leave everything there? The tanks are coated. They'll last for years in the ground, but not exposed like that. Some of them are shedding rust already."

"So what's the difference between that and all the bundles of shingles that lie stashed away under houses while the roofs go on leaking? Except they're out in plain sight."

"Nothing, I guess, except just what you say. You can see them."

"Fine. You just leave them where they are. Don't do a damn thing else. Tell the Chief it's his problem. He said if we got the outfits, they'd do the digging, and they agreed. So it's his problem."

"But nothing will happen."

"I know that. But that bunch of rusting septic tanks will make a first-class monument to my contribution to the Indian problem—whatever that is, and I'm sure I don't know."

"Are you serious?"

"Absolutely."

Bradley turned to go, then hesitated. "There's one other thing."

"What's that?"

"Those people are starting to drink, something fearful. Just about the whole village except for the Chief and his wife."

"That's new, isn't it? I mean they've had a reputation for being a pretty steady lot."

"They've always had a bit of a rumble now and then. But never like it is now. The Chief says it's never been so bad."

"They working?" Arne asked.

"The logging camp is running steady. There's plenty of work and plenty of money. Just about everybody has a job of some kind."

"Maybe they're better off broke. Then they can't buy booze."

"I sometimes think so."

"Well. Sorry I've no answers."

"I just thought I should tell you."

"Okay. And too bad about the septic tanks. Can't win every time."

34

But if Arne couldn't provide answers he still felt compelled to search for them.

He went to Elizabeth Louie. She and her husband, Ben, lived in Kwatsi. Long ago they had been heavy drinkers and Elizabeth often told how they had come to one morning and found their children wandering around the floats in front of the cannery shacks, half clothed and hungry. For some reason that morning they saw their children when they looked at them, though God knows it had been the same for countless previous mornings. They quit, and hadn't had a drop since. Ben tried hard, they both did, and in a good year they took in as much as five thousand dollars during fishing. Then Ben would go in the bush or draw unemployment insurance benefits and they'd scrape through the winter. At least some years they'd do that. Other years, and this was one of them, they'd do poorly in fishing and the jobs seemed to be gone by the time Ben was ready to go logging.

Even though they didn't drink they couldn't hold onto money. They'd get a payout at the season's end of two or three thousand dollars, and the whole family would eat in the café in Davis Bay until it was gone.

So as often as not they were on assistance.

And they'd had their share of grief. One older boy drank himself to death. Another, who got married without the least sense of responsibility toward his wife and the babies which followed one after the other, sat idle in his parents' crowded home as though he had nothing else in mind for the rest of his life.

But this plain little woman had a knack of putting her finger on things occasionally that always took Arne by surprise. She was on the council and had been the only one among them, Arne included, who had foreseen with any accuracy the sense of loss the community would suffer in abandoning the old surroundings. She had favored the move because she saw the hopelessness of staying in Hugger's, but it was a choice between evils. "You are a white man, Mr. Saunders. Any place you go, it's the same for you. But for us, it's different. We belong to one place and we always going to belong to one place. Even a woman gets married to another village, her husband dies and she's going to go back where she belongs."

There was no seeing Elizabeth alone in her house, so Arne picked her up in Davis Bay when she'd finished her shopping one afternoon and drove her home. They sat in the car in front of her place from where one could see, in all its drabness, the hodge-podge of broken windows and car hulks and half-clothed children and littered yards that was Kwatsi.

"Elizabeth, I get a hopeless feeling everything I do now. I didn't think it was going to be any kind of a miracle, moving the people here. But it seems as though there's no good in it at all. Isn't there anything we can do that *would* help?"

She had a way of looking straight ahead when she spoke and forcing out what she had to say as though reciting a prepared speech. But it was never prepared, it was real goods, and sometimes it was cautious because she wasn't sure what Arne was after and other times it was out of her heart so plainly it made her cry, and the tears would find their way down the firmly held face that never looked to the side.

"You done lots for us, Mr. Saunders. We never had no houses like this up Hugger's. These was nice houses when you built them. It's just the people don't know how to look after them. And we never had no running water. And we know you going to get us that sewer sometime.

"I know what it said in that newspaper but you got to understand the people have pretty hard time and they have to say something makes them feel it isn't all their fault."

Arne nodded. "I don't mind that, Elizabeth. Oh, it gets me down a little at the time all right but it doesn't matter. But everybody's life seems so hopeless, the way they drink and neglect the kids and waste anything they get."

Elizabeth waited a long time before she spoke again and Arne averted his eyes from her face to make it easier for her. Then: "I'm going to tell you something I don't say before, Mr. Saunders. You see how bad these people living here and you think it's because they can't make it by Davis Bay. Well I'm going to tell you now. You don't know it but it's just as bad when we was in Hugger's. When the people gettin' their relief in Hugger's and have such hard time to get to store, still they mostly buying just sugar and raisins.

"Some things the people doing in Hugger's, I'm shame to tell you. I can't tell you, some of them things. It's like dogs what they're doing to one another.

"Long as I can remember, the people been drinking like that. Used to be against the law, still they get it from Chinaman at the cannery and anyway, they can make brew any time they like. Some places they say they don't start drinking bad until it's safe to buy it but they been drinking a long time in Hugger's.

"When I'm little girl, them old people still trying to have potlatch. They want to have potlatch and they trying to ask them chiefs from all different villages and even some of them chiefs don't come to potlatch in Hugger's. And when they trying to have potlatch so many them people drinking and spend their money they can't raise enough to make good potlatch. And them old people they so shamed they can't get over it. Them old people die that way, shame inside them so bad. Them old people the ones build them houses in Hugger's. Before that was just long house.

"What I'm going to tell you, you are white man, Mr. Saunders, so anything you try to do, it works for you. You can stay one job all your life cause you know it's going to work for you. You know what you going to do with your money so everything is all right for you.

"But Indians have hard time cause he's not sure what he's going to do. He likes to be just as good as white people but he knows he can't make it. You want people to get steady job, Mr. Saunders, but they know they can't make it."

"But some do, Elizabeth."

"Just few lucky ones. And them ones that drink, Mr. Saunders, they can't help it. They don't want to be like that. They shamed for what they doing to their kids but they can't stop it."

She stopped but she wasn't finished. Arne sensed it in the increasing tightness of her words and he dreaded whatever was left. He did not turn to look because she would be crying in the silent way he knew of her, the tears alone betraying her misery.

Finally: "We trying to be like white people, Mr. Saunders. But we not sure what we going to do."

And Arne kept his eyes averted while she left the car. He did not want to see the silent crying.

35

John Southland from the Victoria office of the Provincial Department of Welfare called to see Arne in the course of a review of that department's responsibility toward Kwatsi. The newspapers had not gone unread.

Arne had known Southland. He'd been one of several professional people whose brains Arne had picked in earlier days—in the days when the jargon of expertise had given him a sense of understanding he now spurned as false, empty, nothing, a puff of words in a wind of confusion.

Tall and spare limbed, Southland ambled as he moved and when he spoke his quizzical turn of mind brought the same sort of ambling quality to his long, large face. And yet he spoke with precision.

They talked awhile around the bits and pieces of their common experience but it wasn't long before the topic began to narrow into the puzzles which Arne so anxiously wanted to resolve. Southland must have seen through him with ease for he unexpectedly cut through Arne's half-conscious preliminaries and put the question squarely.

"What eludes you that you want so badly, Arne? You're so hungry I can smell it. Tie it down for me."

"I'm not sure I'm sure." That was evasive.

"The devil you're not sure. Just be honest. What *really* hangs you up?"

Arne bought a little time to think but it wasn't necessary. And then when he said it, it sounded so paper thin he felt embarrassed by it.

"I don't *know* any Indians. Not one solitary Indian." Then hurriedly: "I'm sorry. That must sound stupid. But it's the truth."

"Fine. But you'll have to go on a little. You can't stop there."

"I'll try. But I was never particularly introspective until this bloody job made me look inside to see what was in there."

"Real can of worms?" It was said with a disarming grin.

"I guess so. We have to go back a bit. You remember I used to eat up a lot of your time and I got pretty good at arguing your own line. You weren't the only one, either.

"Well, I thought I had the picture. I could talk about cultural disintegration and conflicting values and poor role perception. And it really explained the things I thought I saw happening."

"Doesn't it now?"

"It still explains *things*. Maybe. But it doesn't mean I can talk to anybody. It doesn't help me one damn bit, for instance, when some Indians insist that if we provide them with septic tanks, they'll install them, and a year afterwards the tanks are still sitting out in the rain and all the Indians have to say about it is, why won't we dig them in and hook them up."

"You want an Indian to give you a rational explanation for that?"

"No. Not an explanation. But I'd like to be able to talk to the guy on the basis that we would each of us say what we really mean instead of what we think we have to say to each other because of who the other guy is and what we're trying to get out of him."

"Maybe," Southland offered, "you can't have that and be an Indian agent at the same time."

"Good point. Once long ago I got drunk with an Indian. Before I came in the job. It's an awful proposition, but that might have been the most real thing I've ever done with an Indian. I don't remember what we said and it was probably a lot of foolishness but I believe profoundly that it wasn't phoney."

"Now, one more thing. I have always found it easy to talk to Indians who are hard workers and successful in ways that I'd like to be successful in too. In fact I realize now that I've gone to these sort of people for comfort."

"What did you talk about? Mainly, that is."

"That's easy. We knocked those other poor bastards who wouldn't get off their backsides and hack it the way we did. Said there was nothing stopping them, all they had to do was get a job and hang onto it. Well, I don't think it was always as crude as that, you know. But that was the gist of it most of the time."

"You don't call that knowing each other?"

"I call that reinforcing each other's feelings of adequacy. Forgive the near jargon. I don't call it *knowing* each other. But even for what it was, it begs the whole question."

Southland considered that, then: "And the question?"

Arne leaned forward and hammered each word out for he had found at last exactly what to say: "*How do you talk to a man who doesn't share your notions about work or money or wife or kids or house or sanitation or what the hell he's going to live on tomorrow or next year and reach him where he's really alive inside and he can reach you back?*"

He fixed Southland's eyes for the answer and Southland obliged: "I don't know."

"Join the club. I think I get close with one poor little woman who feels so bad for the people sometimes she cries, but I haven't the guts to look her in the face and go on with it."

Arne began spinning paper clips and Southland retrieved one that spun off. Then he made an offer to Arne. "I can't help you on the communication bit. I can give you a nice pat piece of jargon to cover it but you wouldn't want that. But I can give you a point of view which may put the failure of houses and roads and water systems into some perspective."

"Try me. I'll listen to anything."

"All right. First off, the guts of what grinds at Indians from day to day isn't something peculiar to Indians. It's poverty, plain, simple and intractable. Oh, there are many who car about aboriginal rights and the land question and broken treaties, and these are specifically Indian issues. But most of the caring is done by otherwise successful people. But what is called the Indian problem is no more Indian than tuberculosis is Indian. For historical reasons Indians got more than a share of both, but that doesn't change the nature of the disease.

"Poverty is poverty, whoever suffers it. And you can get into some fearfully involved arguments about what poverty is and isn't, so right off let's be clear I'm not talking about poverty anywhere but here and now and where we're at.

"Now, it's more than just economic hardship. Economic hardship is part of it and if that were all, it would be easily solved. Money would cure it. But poverty is failure and you can't buy off failure.

"I think you have to see it in terms of an individual and groups of individuals having to live, as part of a total population, in a particular environment. Put aside the questions of fairness or justice or good or bad elements in the environment for a moment. You might have your doubts about an environment that includes underarm deodorants and electric-powered tooth-brushes, but if you want to cut through to basic principles you can't get hung up on the peripherals.

"Individuals and groups within a total population either interact effectively with an environment and thrive, or interact ineffectively and fail. And if the environment changes radically, individuals and groups and total populations develop new kinds of effectiveness or suffer.

"Man's environments are social and economic as well as physical and all rather intricately bound up. The land and sea are the same land and sea as they were before the white man came but the total environment is as changed as day from night.

"Effectiveness is the key and if the simplicity of that leads you to think I'm about to render the secret in a dazzle of illumination, I'm sorry. I don't know what effectiveness *is*, I can only describe what I see of it as it shows up in how people live.

"Regular employment in the production of goods and services is the main avenue to participation in the abundant social and economic environment of our time and place—and it is abundant as man's environments go.

"But there's a whole life style of success which has to be seen of a piece: compliance with the daily and weekly timetable of industry; the will to postpone satisfactions; personal and family budgeting; healthy personal relationships in home, workplace and school; tolerable personal and household cleanliness; using birth control to keep the number of dependent children within the capacity to support them.

"By the same token, there's a life style of failure—or poverty, if you prefer. It is a life style of ineffectiveness and it is self-reinforcing. The ineffectiveness that underlies the life style is sustained and entrenched by the life style itself.

"We know it: irregular living patterns; poor to hopeless management of personal and family resources; badly strained personal relationships; neglect of children; excessive drinking; resort to violence to settle disputes, especially husband against wife; dirt and squalor; no tolerance for the boredom of employment; no maintenance of physical facilities like housing or clothing or furnishings; no capacity to make birth control work; high illegitimacy rates."

Arne had moved to the window where he stared out at the grayness of a summer rain. The mist hung in the tree tops. But his attention had not wandered. "You're describing Kwatsi," he observed.

"Indeed. And I'm describing a hundred others just as well."

"Go on. You make sense in my limited experience."

"Poverty is not simply unemployment, and opportunity for employment won't solve it. Low income is the product of the life style yet we still think of it as the cause. The whole life style is an impediment to using employment to earn income. Then the life style wastes what income is available. In fact we sometimes see the anomaly of a family that will order their living just enough to accommodate employment but maintain virtually all the other ingredients of the poverty life style. On the same income other families will live the life style of success." Arne broke in. "You're telling me that poverty is a way of life, not an economic circumstance."

"That's part of what I'm trying to say, yes."

Arne went on: "But suppose we assume that people who live one way of life can't really judge another way of life. That maybe people who don't work, who ruin their houses, drink, beat their wives, neglect their kids—all in our terms of course, they wouldn't describe it that way themselves—are satisfied with how it is. Why should we get in a sweat to change them?"

"I think I can make a case for us being in a sweat all right. But before I go any further, have you got birth and death data on the group in Kwatsi for, say, the past twenty years?"

"I would have. We have copies of all the vital statistics registrations. What do you want to know?"

"Basic stuff. How many births, how many deaths. What ages of death, causes. That kind of thing. Tell you what. I have to keep a couple of other appointments but I'd like to see you again tomorrow morning. You go through these registrations and organize the data any way you like. You tell me what it tells you."

"You're on. When tomorrow morning?"

"Nine o'clock?"

"Done."

Southland ambled out.

36

It was uncanny the way the image of Kwatsi that had grown by accretion in Arne's mind from his encounters now climbed in identical substance out of the dry facts recorded in the cumbersome bound volumes of birth and death registrations.

By the time Southland joined him at nine in the morning he had tallied the data into a dozen startling statements, having only to decide which were the more telling.

"Well?"

"An interesting exercise. Would you like it delivered with my best facsimile of academic detachment or shall I give it flesh and blood after my naturally unscientific bias?"

"You have some feelings about it?"

"Feelings? Yes. I feel guilty that I can deal on paper with the misery of a people I actually know and talk to and do so bloody little about it."

"We haven't established yet that there is anything you can do. So give me the facts. They won't tell us anything we don't already know but they'll prevent us taking refuge in academic fancies."

"All right. There are just over two hundred and twenty people alive in this group now.

"In the past eighteen years, sixty-nine people have died. One death for just a shade over every three people presently alive." Arne looked up from his notes. He wanted a better way to put it. "How many communities in Canada of two hundred and twenty people have had sixty-nine funerals in the last eighteen years?"

Southland nodded. "Go on."

"Only twelve of those deaths were of people over fifty. Only one person in six makes it past fifty.

"Forty-five of those sixty-nine people who died in that time, died between birth and ten years." Again Arne looked up. "Sixty-five percent of the coffins were child size."

"Yes."

"In that eighteen years, one hundred and sixty-eight children were born. Forty-three of them have died. Of every four born, one dies while yet a child."

"What have you on causes of death?"

"In the birth to ten years group, seventeen of pneumonia, six of burns, six of drowning and sixteen by a variety of other causes."

Southland observed: "The frequency of pneumonia as a cause of death is a remarkably accurate index of child neglect. Go on."

"In four cases the medical certificate specifically mentions malnutrition. Now I've got one more here, but it involves a judgment on my part. I don't know if I should use it."

"What kind of judgment?"

"The question of physical care. How many child deaths were basically from physical neglect."

"Would you say willful neglect?"

"No. Willful implies the power to choose to do better. I do not any longer believe these people have that power."

"Then go ahead with your judgment."

"I am saying that seventy-five per cent of the child deaths would not have occurred if there had been effective physical care."

Arne waited after he said that while Southland visibly thought about it. Southland commented only to say that it was highly probable.

Arne went on. "Just one more. There was only one death between ten and twenty years of age. But in the age group twenty to sixty years, there were twelve deaths. Four were drownings, one was a violent accident I wouldn't care to describe, two were suffocation on vomit and one was alcohol poisoning—and in each of those eight, alcohol was the decisive factor. The other four were different illnesses which aren't necessarily related to, what shall I say, the way of life?" He made it sound like a question.

"Tell us in fact how a people die and we can tell you how a people live," Southland answered, and now he shifted in his chair as if preparing to go on with the argument he had suspended the day before. "I think we have to be concerned. There is too much grief to shrug off with a that's-their-way-of-life-don't-make-judgments-about-it kind of argument. But what to do? Change the way of life? Yes. But how?

"It would be so easy if it were just a matter of money. Provide good houses and enough of them, provide roads and water and sewer and power. Provide a generous income.

"But this is trying to buy for people what they lack the effectiveness to achieve through their own interaction with the social and economic environment. Providing the products of success won't change the life style of people who cannot secure those products for themselves. Life is not a question just of consuming goods. It is a question also of directing oneself in self-sustaining, not self-destructive, ways."

"But damn it, man," Arne interjected, "surely if you do provide a decent physical environment and a chance to go to school, the kids'll change. Maybe in a couple of generations. After all, we've never really done a complete overhaul in any one community. There's always so much more to do than there is money to do it with."

Southland absorbed the frustration in Arne's outburst. "Do you *really* think you've seen anything that should convince you of that? Is it behavior of the people which produces the squalid physical surroundings or the squalid physical surroundings which produces the behavior of the people?"

"But if you're born into it..."

"Ah, yes. If you are born into it. The chain of poverty. Erroneously thinking of poverty as material insufficiency resulting in adverse behavior patterns, we say we will break the chain of poverty by improving the physical environment into which the children of poverty are born.

"But, you see, it is the behavior, the life style into which the child is born that renders him ineffective, quite apart from any defect he might inherit. If we have learned one thing about the infant, it surely is that the crucial source of health for the personality is in the warmth of physical and emotional love the mother lavishes on the newborn babe.

"There it is in that primal relationship that you build or botch the personality for all the subsequent relationships and effectiveness in life. That is where poverty reproduces itself. Exhausted by all those unwanted pregnancies, her relationship with her man strained at the best of times, her days and nights turbulent with her own drinking or at any rate of those around her, what has she left to give? Her girls grow up to be like herself and her sons to be the kind of men who come and go in her own life.

"You speak of education. But you see it takes as much effectiveness to interact successfully in that part of the environment as in any other. It may be a place where youngsters can learn how to put their effectiveness to work, it's not a place where they can be given it if they don't have it."

Arne's frustration spilled over. "But what the hell are you saying? That we shouldn't bother with all this housing and physical services? Or education or anything else?"

"No. I don't say that. In fact I heartily support it. Build houses and all the rest of it. All you can. And issue social assistance to people whose behavior is incompatible with going to work. And keep kids in school as much as you can. Just don't imagine that any of it will alter the life style. Oh, you'll see some change in some people. There's no doubt of that. But not enough, I'm afraid, to make any impact on the volume of poverty."

"But what happens?" Arne demanded. "In spite of the high death rate, the birth rate is even greater. These groups of people in poverty are growing at a much faster rate than the rest of the population. Where does that lead us?"

"Frankly, I don't know."

"All right. One more thing. What about the high rate of births to unmarried mothers, and I don't mean just unmarried legally. I mean girls having a child every year and no enduring relationship with any man. I get the feeling this is maybe the worst feature of all but I hesitate to judge for fear all I'm doing is imposing my own morality. This is where a lot of the social assistance goes, and there's no point suggesting these girls should be working. They've got a full-time job looking after their kids."

"I should say that bearing children outside an enduring relationship with a man is a pretty ineffective way to function. It implies individual ineffectiveness on both the mother's and the father's part and it is not surprising that it occurs most frequently in groups and communities where the lack of effectiveness is evident in many different ways."

Arne summarized. "So if I read you correctly, you're saying that what I have been hammering at is not an Indian problem specifically but a poverty problem, that poverty is a way of life, that it is rooted in ineffectiveness, however derived, and that nobody really knows how you change life styles."

"Because we don't know how to give effectiveness to people who don't have it."

"Well, let's quit before we go around that circle again."

37

Sammy couldn't figure why the police said it was his fault about the baby, and that's what he said when the lawyer from the legal aid came to see them. Lots of times babies died when they got sick, and anyway it was the women looked after the kids, not the men. After he said that he didn't say any more and so the lawyer had to talk to Eliza and Winnifred and Sammy gave up even listening to what they were saying. He wished he could get away and get some wine from somewhere. He felt empty all over, not like he was hungry but empty all over inside, everywhere. It was the feeling he got when he most needed to drink something.

Finally the lawyer went away and Sammy went to the Willies' house to see if they were drinking anything. The old woman's pension check must be all gone because it was past the end of the month, but they'd got their relief and they might have some wine from that.

But they didn't have anything and after Sammy sat in their house for a while, he figured they didn't expect to get any so he left.

He went to Herbie Sam's place. He didn't like to go there because of Herbie and Eliza but he could nearly always get a drink from Herbie. It was like Herbie owed it to him for having Eliza when he wanted. Sammy couldn't stop him but still he guessed Herbie felt like he was doing something wrong and he'd let Sammy have stuff to make up for it.

This time there was a bunch drinking in Herbie's. There was Ron Charlie and Edna and Sammy's brother Jimmy and some others. When Sammy came in he sat on the floor just inside the door and Herbie's wife, Leona, poured a cupful of wine and passed it to him.

Everybody was drunk and talking loud and Sammy didn't say anything. Even when he was drunk he didn't get as loud as most people and he didn't fight except sometimes he'd go after Eliza and try to straighten her around a bit, but it never did much good. He wished he'd got a better woman.

After a while David Jimmy came to the door but Herbie told him he couldn't come in. Sammy figured there couldn't be much wine left because Herbie would have let David in if he wasn't trying to save the wine for himself and the ones who were already there. It was all right to tell David to go away because everybody knew he would keep his wine just for himself and only one or two others, whenever he got any. It was no good like that when a man wouldn't share up. Only it was all right if you just had a little left and there were too many drinking on it already. Then you could close your door because otherwise everybody just got half drunk and that was no good if you couldn't get any more.

Herbie could tell David to keep out because David knew Herbie could lick him. One time Sammy had tried to keep David out of his house. Sammy had locked the door and when David said to let him in Sammy had told him to go away because he didn't have any wine to share. He told David to go drink his own wine. David couldn't break the door so he broke the window. But Sammy had shoved a chair up so he couldn't make it in that window and David came around and broke in a window at the back, before Sammy could stop him. He'd got pretty rough with Sammy then, so after that any time he came Sammy would let him in.

Sammy had been right when he guessed there wasn't much wine left because pretty soon Herbie passed around some more and finished the last of a bottle himself and said that was it. Sammy'd had a third cupful by then and he felt pretty good but he knew he'd have to get some more or the empty feeling would come on him worse than ever.

Ron was pretty drunk and started to fight with Herbie. He said Herbie was holding out on them, and Herbie told him to shut his goddamn face and after a while they were hitting at each other but they were too drunk to do any harm. Edna tried to help Ron and so Leona got fighting with Edna and then Sammy left. He figured he'd go to town and see if he could get some wine.

Sammy walked along the edge of the road to town. The road left the shore and went straight through some bush for a way, then followed the shore again into Davis Bay. Long ago there'd been a trail along the edge of the rocks but nobody used it any more and you could only just make it out. Sammy knew it was there since his dad had brought him to Kwatsi once to dig clams, but some of the young people didn't even know it was there. It went by a place where there was hardly any beach, just a high place where the rocks went straight into the water way below. Sometimes Sammy walked that way just to see the old trail. It was like it used to be, and he could forget the houses at Kwatsi and the people, and it was just like it was years ago, and his dad was still with him.

When he got to the store they told him all his relief was used up and he couldn't have anything more till the fifteenth. Some got their relief at the first and some at the fifteenth. Sammy couldn't figure why he got his at the fifteenth. The ones who got theirs on the first already had it but now he had to wait to the fifteenth.

He got hold of Mr. Garber and told him they were out of everything at the house. Mr. Garber said the same thing, that they'd got all their relief. That was the trouble with the agent sending it to the store. He asked if he could maybe get a little stuff ahead off next month and Mr. Garber said no and then Sammy said just a little bread and some milk and maybe a few little things for the kids cause they were pretty hungry and then Mr. Garber told the girl to let Sammy take five dollars' worth and to mark it down.

Sammy got a dollar for the bag of grub from a white guy in the beer parlor and that was just enough to get a quart bottle of wine. He'd hoped to get a half gallon, but a dollar was all the white guy would give him for the grub.

38

Sammy felt ashamed about not taking his wine into the village to share but lately he'd got so he was afraid of the empty feeling afterward if he didn't get enough to get really drunk and pass out. It didn't use to be like that but now he couldn't help it, he had to keep it for himself if he only got a small bottle.

So when he came to the place where the road left the beach he went along the sand, then climbed the bank to the trail that followed along the rocks where the beach petered out. When he came to the highest place he sat on the ground with his back against a stump and started to drink the wine. He could look out over the sea while he drank. The tide had been out and was flooding back in and a low swell coming in from the open strait made the water surge and eddy against the rocks below.

It was like his dad's fishing place on the river that came into Hugger's Inlet at the people's proper home. There was a back eddy in the river and a high rock overhanging the pool. You could stand on a rock and see the salmon in the swirling water below, milling and swimming around while they waited to go on up the river to spawn. His dad would heft the long gaff skillfully up and down, then drive it suddenly into the swirling water and bring out the sockeye. The fish would thrash wildly on the gaff hook that came away from the shaft to hang by a thong.

That was the best gaff fishing place on the river and there was a place that went with it just up a ways to set nets or build a trap. Sammy knew the story about that place. His dad told him the story many times when he was a boy.

The first Matsatenok man had the form of a wolf and he had to find a place to live with his three children. He travelled until he came to a place not far from where the river came into the inlet. His brother was with him and they argued about who should have this place.

To settle the argument they stood apart and threw a magic rock back and forth to see who was the most powerful and finally the brother missed the rock and the first, who turned into his proper human form, claimed the place. But his brother was angry and stole one of the children, tearing it in many pieces which turned into feathers and became birds to fly over all the earth.

The Matsatenok people descended from the two children who survived, and the rock which the brother missed stayed where it fell, overlooking the pool where Sammy's dad came to have his fishing place, handed down to him from his fathers before him.

There'd been trouble over the fishing place. Sammy never

understood about it really. Some of the chiefs claimed his father hadn't made good his right to the place because he hadn't upheld his name in the potlatch. One of the big chiefs gave a potlatch once and Sammy was a small boy in the big house. There were many people in the big house, all gathered around the sides and in the center was a big fire. The fire threw light on the faces of the people but in the far corners of the building everything was dark, and Sammy was scared in the big house when he was a small boy.

And that one time he remembered, one of the chiefs spoke about his dad and some of the others who were the younger men in those days, and he called them down in front of the people because they hadn't put anything toward the potlatch and accused them of spending their money from fishing on drink and just for themselves.

His dad drank a lot and it got worse after that, and they used to have a hard time in the winter. They lived in one corner of a big house that belonged to Sammy's uncle and his mother used to go every night to dig clams when the tide was low. Other times they had to eat just what little dried fish Sammy's uncle spared them.

When his dad died some of the men said he'd never made his name good, he'd never potlatched in his own right, but Sammy went on using the fishing place. He liked to stand out on the very edge of the rock and stare into the swirling water. It was as though his eyes were drawn right into the water until finally he would make out the shape of the salmon. He would begin to move the gaff up and down then, slowly at first, but a little faster as the salmon took shape to his eyes and then it was as though a spirit took his arm and drove the shaft, for suddenly it would plunge into the water and he would grab it with both hands to hold the writhing sockeye that fought to get free of the hook.

But he felt the shame of what the old people said, though he understood only a little of the failing of his father in the potlatch. And he understood even less of the mysteries of the winter ceremonies that had died out during his time as a boy, but the fear of the Tsonkwa stayed with him and got mixed with the shame of his father and sometimes at night alone in the dark he wanted to run from the shame and the fear. Sammy drank some more of the wine and thought still of those times that were so long gone by.

He wished they hadn't made him marry Eliza. The people didn't fix the marrying now the way they used to. But his mother had made it with Eliza's people that he marry her and he had to go through with it. They lived for a while with her people but after she had her second child they stayed in a shed with Sammy's mother. Eliza wasn't a good woman like his mother. She wouldn't go to the beach if the clam tide came late at night. She'd stay in her bed while the old woman went out with the clam fork and the bucket to get clams so they could eat.

When he went to gill net at Rivers Inlet in the summer he had to take her with him because already Herbie Sam was fooling around with her. But she got drinking at Rivers Inlet and he had more trouble with her there so finally he left her behind in Hugger's. It was better Herbie than all those guys at Rivers Inlet, white guys and Chinamen at the cannery.

He wished Herbie wouldn't talk about it, but when Herbie got drunk he'd start talking about who'd made Eliza's kids, him or Sammy. Sammy couldn't stop him because Herbie was about the toughest man in the whole village. Just about everybody had fought with him but nobody'd ever beat him and sometimes he hurt some of the others pretty bad. Sometimes when he was drunk he'd try to get Sammy to fight. He'd laugh about who was going to make Eliza's next baby and Sammy would just get away from him. But when Herbie was sober he seemed like he knew he owed something to Sammy and he'd never see Sammy stuck for grub or anything. He'd nearly always share his drink, even though he'd want to fight after they got drunk.

Sammy saw that the wine was nearly gone so he put the bottle down between his feet to look at it awhile before he finished it. Then he looked out toward the sea again. In the distance he could make out the fish boats off the mouth of the bay.

It was a long time since he'd fished now. He couldn't remember how long. But the company quit letting him have a rental boat while they were up in Hugger's. They said he was too far in the hole and they were losing money on him. He didn't believe it though. They just picked on some guys and they'd cheat them on the books and finally cut them off. They picked on Sammy because he couldn't understand the books himself.

Maybe next year he'd get a boat. He could fish, same as anybody. Maybe he'd go to Rivers Inlet and if there was a good run of sockeye he'd make enough to buy his own boat. He'd never owned a boat, but if he had his own boat they couldn't cut him off.

Sammy felt pretty good now. The wine had settled all over him and there was no empty feeling any longer. He knew he was almost drunk and he took up the bottle again and looked at how much was left. There was still most of the bottom part and he drank this all at once so it would do the most good. After a while he knew he was pretty drunk and he didn't feel ashamed any more for not sharing the wine with someone.

When he got up he looked down from the edge of the rock to where the tide had risen over the boulders and begun to creep up the rock face far below. It was just like the old fishing place as the swells brought the sea in to swirl over the rocks and against the rock face.

The swirling waters drew his eyes and after a long time he could make out the salmon as they milled around, waiting to go up the river to spawn.

But they were laughing at him from under the swirling surface of the water, laughing as the water drew his eyes down into the deep places full of salmon.

He hefted the shaft, up and down, up and down, and then his arm, like his eye, was taken and the gaff plunged into the midst of the salmon in the swirling water.

They found his body the next morning lodged in the rocks where the receding tide had left it.

39

It was Corporal Thompson, with Dyke to help him, who went below the rock bluff in a seine boat skiff and scrambled over the seaweed and the boulders to fetch the body. Arne, en route to Kwatsi on other business, joined the group of villagers who waited at the confluence of the beach and road for Thompson's return and was told of the drowning.

"He falls in from high place on rock I guess."

"I see." And I know what else, Arne thought, for it is always the same. He was drunk and he fell in and he drowned, and he was either alone or whoever was with him was too drunk to help him. Arne was about to put questions to verify these assumptions then thought better of it—for what possible use could it serve.

When the skiff grounded on the beach the men waded in and dragged it up. Then, when Thompson and Dyke had stepped out, they carried the skiff with the body up to the road and the RCMP van.

While Dyke directed the transfer of the body from the skiff to the vehicle Arne and Thompson exchanged brief words.

"The family knows?"

"Yes. Some kids saw him and went to Billy. He phoned us and he said he was going to Eliza right away."

"Drunk?"

"There was an empty wine bottle at the top of the bluff. The autopsy will confirm it but I haven't seen a drowning of this type yet where alcohol wasn't the main factor."

Arne thought about the gleanings from his death registrations and the too-present sense of despair gnawed again at his hopes for Kwatsi. "I don't know what to do about the drinking," he said, as though the recital of the obvious really mattered enough to be said. "I don't know how to move the mountain or empty out the river or dry up all the ocean. I don't know."

"Nobody does and don't let any bloody fool tell you otherwise."

"What about the charges against Eliza now?"

"This is the end of that. No difficulty now in withdrawing. Just a statement that in view of Sammy's death no useful purpose would be served by continuing against Eliza. I don't know what Sammy solved for himself when he fell in the chuck, but he solved that much for me."

The body was loaded and Dyke waited to go. Thompson joined him and Arne gathered all the villagers into his car and drove into Kwatsi, letting them out by the Chief's house.

He went in then to see Billy. "You know 'bout Sammy?" the Chief asked him.

"Yes."

"You have to give them people coffin for Sammy, you know. They got nothing."

"I'll look after that."

They sat in silence then in the dinginess of Billy's house and Arne thought about but put aside the errand which had brought him: what to do about a man who desperately needed a house for his family, whom regulations required to contribute 135 dollars in order to qualify for an 8500-dollar subsidy and who had contributed so far absolutely not one penny and shown no signs of doing so this side of eternity. In fairness to Kwatsi it had not happened yet in the program there, but every place had its first.

But this morning it could wait and Arne let the silence exist, something it had taken him a long time to learn to do. When Billy would break it one of two things would be clear: what Billy really wanted to talk about, or that Billy didn't really want to talk.

Then: "We got to stop them white guys comin' in here, you know."

"But how, Billy?" Arne had been around this circle before and he knew how thoroughly Corporal Thompson had also. It was cruel to throw it back at Billy like that, but he felt it was the only chance Billy had to recognize the impossibility of what he was asking.

"Maybe we gonna make a bylaw. We make a bylaw, no white guys after ten o'clock. We use that Indian Act where we can make bylaws, you know."

"But Billy, the Act says you can make bylaws for certain definite things and that's not one of them. It always comes back to the people themselves. If they don't *want* those guys we can keep them out. But you come right down to it, they're not prepared to tell those guys to stay out."

"There was white guys that night Sammy's baby died, you know. Thompson takes Sammy to court on that, but he don't take those white guys. It was those white guys had them drinkin' that night, you know."

"But they wouldn't tell Thompson those guys' names."

The silence took over again but this time Arne couldn't stand it. It was heavy with the agony of his impotence, and the unfairness to both of them that Billy had no basis for understanding it. So he broke it: "Have you tried talking to these white men yourself? They must have a conscience buried in them somewhere."

Billy looked directly at him. "When these people drinkin' I don't go out, you know. Whether there's white guys around or not. I'm old man now, you know. I go out when these people drinkin', they beat me up, you know."

"I'm sorry, Billy. I didn't know." And inside, what the hell else could I say? What does anybody say when an old man sits there and lets you know he lives in fear of the street in his own village, of the violence of his own kin?

Billy motioned toward the door. "I lock my door when they drinkin'. Still they breakin' it down sometimes, you know. They kickin' it in and raisin' hell with me, you know." The door had been shattered and repaired, and the frame was sprung where the lock had been forced.

Arne had nothing left. Inside in the reaches of his despair the words that recurred so habitually now repeated themselves once more: I don't know what to do. I don't know, I don't know, I don't know.

40

T his visit that did not have any answers came to an end when a young man, or older boy depending on how you looked at him, called to say he wanted to see Arne. Arne excused himself from Billy and went out with the youngster to the car for privacy.

He was Jacob Sam, one of Herbie's, and Arne knew him. He'd gone to school in Hugger's, then started high school in the boarding home program in the lower mainland, and quit. The family who'd boarded him had found him pleasant but unreach-able and his teachers had thought him unresponsive at best, dull at worst.

Perhaps he was a classic case of what an Indian day school couldn't do in the isolation of Hugger's Inlet or perhaps the problem reached a long way back into the unknowns of his ancestral origins.

School not being useful to him, he had been offered upgrad-ing in a program specifically designed for students with his kind of experience, to be followed by trade training if he wished.

He didn't wish, not for the upgrading and not for the trade training.

The alternatives to that were few but they did exist. The logging outfits had jobs where willing men could start without experience.

Willing. What is willing? Who wills and why?

Jacob Sam was nineteen now and had never had a work experience of so much as eight hours duration as far as Arne could discover, and he'd made a point on one occasion of so trying to discover.

They settled in the car. "Well, Jacob? What can I do for you today?"

"I wonder could I get a little relief."

"I see. Are you staying with your dad? Generally the rule is that a young single person is part of the household he stays in, and if your dad qualified for assistance we'd include you. And if he didn't, we wouldn't issue anything."

Then the wait and the doubts. Does he understand that? What hasn't he told me yet? Was that too negative? Arne decided it had been a little preclusive. "Is there a particular problem?"

"I ain't single no more."

"I see." Arne reached for a notebook. Now the careful ques-tion. How not to offend? "I'll just get a note here. There's yourself. Jacob Sam. How old are you, Jacob?" He knew but it helped to establish the routine.

"Nineteen. Twenty next month, I guess."

"Okay. Now who are you responsible for?" Not married to or living with. Don't know that yet.

"Janet."

"Janet...?"

"Janet Charlie."

"I see. How old is Janet? Damn. Shouldn't have asked that. He won't know. Quickly. "Janet Charlie. Who's her dad, and I'll just get her particulars here from the band list."

"Alfred Charlie."

Arne located the family on the list. "Janet. Twelfth of June, 1954. That makes her fifteen. Guess that's right, eh?"

"Guess so."

"Married yet?"

"Gonna get married next year."

"I see. Where are you staying?"

"Her dad's place. But them people say we got to get our own relief."

Arne put away the band list but kept the notebook open. "Been together long?"

"Since last winter."

"So it's a definite arrangement."

"Yeh."

What do you say that will be of some use? What do you say, Arne Saunders, you who would get a job and buy an axe and build a cabin out of the timber that stands there on the reserve for the taking, if it was you. But you wouldn't, you know, if it was you, because if you were Jacob it would all be hopeless or something else so inexplicably different from what it would be for you that you cannot guess at it, so what do you say?

In the event he said: "Have you tried to get a job?"

"I can't get no job."

"Have you *really* tried?"

"Yeh, I been there. But they don't want nobody hasn't got experience."

And Arne imagined how it was in the hiring office: the expressionless face and the cheap teenage clothing and especially the utterly useless boots that had been bought for their brassy buttons and patent narrow toes with the jazzy small squared ends, all these taken in and rapidly assessed and the stock answer given coldly, nothing just now, maybe in a month or so.

Yes, Arne Saunders, what do you know of that, you who could

have turned up the palms of your hands when you were fifteen and shown callouses hard and thick and yellow and you'd have been grabbed in that hiring office before some other outfit made you a better offer. What, really, can you know?

"Janet going to have a baby?"

"Pretty quick I guess."

"It's a lot of responsibility. Babies come along awfully fast."

"Can't help that I guess."

No, I guess you can't, Arne thought, then went on thinking about a young couple starting married life in a corner of the old people's place which was, as a matter of plain fact, where most married life in Kwatsi did start.

Jacob perhaps thought of it too. At any rate he put a related question: "When you gonna build me a house?"

"Let me explain how that works. First off, only so much money comes to Kwatsi each year for houses. This year, four. Next year, four again, we hope."

"I thought everybody was supposed to get a house soon's they moved here." There was something akin to sullen hostility in the way it was said. Arne ignored that, dealt only with the statement.

"No," he said. "That wasn't quite it. We said it would take time and new families have formed since the move, faster than we can keep up."

"Them other villages gettin' all the houses. They say Yucla gettin' ten houses this year."

"Yes. That's right. But we did a careful survey and they had just that much more need for houses. They had two and a half times as many families without houses as Kwatsi."

"What d'ya have to do? Go join those people at Yucla?"

"That would be up to you. But the way it works now is that when your band council decides you're next for help with housing, we go to the schedule and work out from your income how much contribution you have to make and how much subsidy you get. In your case, with income less than 3000 a year, it would be 135 dollars from you and up to an 8500-dollar subsidy. For that you can build an adequate little home without a basement. But first you have to see the council."

"They ain't gonna do nothin' for me. I might as well quit this village."

Arne sighed. "Up to you, Jacob."

Arne reached again into his brief case. "Here's an application form. Fill it out. I'll be back in the village this afternoon and you can give it to me."

"When do I get some relief?"

"After I get your application."

Jacob left the car and Arne watched him slouch along toward his in-laws.

Jacob, you have just taken the last shred of fight out of me but you, you poor bastard, never had any to start with.

You're nineteen and you're dead already.

AFTERWORD

AFTERWORD:
Who Are These People
We Call Indians?

W ho are these people we call Indians? If we are to support
separate programs, different solutions, special rights
and other distinctions, should we not try to grasp the difference
between Indians and others which account for these? Although
a very real difference, it is neither uniform nor static. It varies
enormously from person to person and from place to place, and
just when you think you understand it, it changes in front of
your eyes.

Before Columbus, a dark-skinned people with straight, black
hair occupied the Americas. They lived mainly in tribal groups
and clans, practicing a stone-age economy based for the most
part on hunting, fishing and gathering. They were more often
nomadic than sedentary, living for much of the year in extended
family groups and small bands. Many language groups and a
proliferation of dialects prevailed. The nation state as it existed
in Europe at the time of Columbus did not exist, even in a
rudimentary form, in the territory that is now Canada.

The greater part of these people, called Indians by the Europeans on discovery, had been in the Americas for many thou-

sands of years. In the Arctic fringe, a smaller scattering of different people, labelled Eskimos on discovery by Europeans, had arrived somewhat more recently through Arctic Siberia.

Five hundred years after Columbus, the descendants of these "Indians" are an extremely various people, now virtually entirely of mixed ancestry and owing their genetic inheritance as much to the European occupiers (and occasional modern Asian) as to the Aboriginal ancestors with whom many of them prefer to identify.

Understanding is not made easier by the profusion of terms, each with potentially different meanings, depending on who speaks and who listens, by which we refer to these people. We hear variously of Indians, of natives, of First Nations people, of status Indians and non-status Indians, of urban Indians, of treaty Indians and non-treaty Indians, of off-reserve and on-reserve Indians, of Metis and, not so frequently now but once commonly and seldom with much respect, of half-breeds. We now increasingly hear of Aboriginal people, a term used historically by anthropologists.

In fact, the term Aboriginal, in application to all people who descend wholly or in part from the original inhabitants, whether Indian or Inuit, in Canada or Asia or Europe, appears to have become preferred in most usage.

When the European occupier first arrived, distinction between the races was easy. Those already here were strikingly different in appearance, dress, language and lifestyle from the people who came on the ships.

Genetic and cultural mixing got underway rapidly, however, and in time government found it necessary to define in law who was an Indian. Without definition, it would be impossible to know with certainty who, among an increasingly mixed people, were to be subject to legislated benefits or disabilities, to reside on reserves set aside for Indians, for example, or to be forbidden alcohol.

Membership in a recognized Indian band was a closely related issue. If a reserve of land were to be set aside for the Squamish Band, there had to be a definition in law of who was an Indian and who, among Indians, was entitled to membership in the Squamish Band and hence to share in the reserve.

When we speak, then, of a status Indian, we mean someone who has Indian status according to the Indian Act of Canada. A non-status Indian is almost always someone of mixed ancestry who is concerned to be identified as an Indian but who, for one of a variety of reasons, does not have status under the Indian Act.

A treaty Indian is a status Indian who is a member of a band which was a signatory to one of a series of treaties established between the crown and, mainly, the eastern and great plains tribes during the eighteenth, nineteenth and early twentieth centuries. A non-treaty Indian is a status Indian who is not a member of a band which entered into one of the historic treaties. The great majority of the status Indians in British Columbia are non-treaty Indians; most of the eastern and great plains status Indians are treaty Indians.

The term non-treaty Indian is often confused with the term non-status Indian.

An on-reserve Indian is simply a status Indian who lives on an Indian reserve, a tract of land to which title remains vested in the federal crown but which is set aside for the use and benefit of a band (very occasionally in common for more than one band). An off-reserve Indian is generally understood to be a status Indian who has taken up residence somewhere other than a reserve, although the term is sometimes used to refer to a non-status Indian.

Generally the term refers to individuals and families living here and there in non-Indian communities, not whole communities of status Indians living off-reserve. There are a number of status Indian communities situated on crown lands, both federal and provincial, which are not reserves but these resemble reserve communities in most other respects. The term off-reserve Indian is not usefully descriptive of a member of this sort of community.

(I see I have now used the term non-Indian. When you have dealt a long time with the subject of Indians of every sort, you may have many terms for the numerous categories of Indians but all other people tend to be simply non-Indians or, in the vernacular, white guys.)

You can see already that the term Indian needs qualification if meaning is to be reasonably specific: the term native suffers difficulty, too. The term, "he's native" probably means "he's Indian" which most likely means "he's of mixed ancestry and the Indian in him is evident and he might or might not be status". Of course we also use the term in reference to white guys, for example when we say someone is a native of Toronto (poor bloke), but there is generally little confusion here with the use of the term in relation to people of Indian ancestry.

Very few terms are used to refer to someone in whom we wish specifically to identify the condition of mixed ancestry.

It is not uncommon and in the main respectful to say of such a person that she is part native; it is not generally respectful to say of her that she is a half-breed or a breed, although the latter terms have been, at some times and in some regions, used without disrespect. Former versions of the Indian Act have used the term half-breed to describe persons of mixed ancestry.

The Metis are a people of a specific mixed ancestry brought about by the union of the French voyageur with Indian women, and who settled in the Red River district, mainly following 1820. It is confusing to refer to other people of mixed Indian and European ancestry as Metis. Most Metis today are found still in the prairie provinces although certain people of mixed ancestry in the Mackenzie Valley of the Northwest Territories are also recognized as Metis. In 1982, the Canadian Parliament recognized the Metis as one of the Aboriginal people of Canada. This illustrates the confusing but persistent practice of recognizing people of mixed ancestry as Aboriginal, equally with those persons, rare now if existing at all, who are fully Aboriginal.

Urban Indians are status or non-status Indians who live in one of the larger cities. Particularly with respect to status Indians, debate has developed about who should be responsible for programs to assist these people. The federal government accepts responsibility for Indians on reserves and on crown lands but contends that the province or municipality should extend services on the same basis as to other citizens when status Indians live in municipalities or other non-native communities. Some provinces and municipalities dispute this, saying they do not have sufficient revenues and that Indians in any case are a federal responsibility irrespective of where they live.

Significantly large numbers of Indian people now do live in cities. Winnipeg is said to contain more Indian people than any exclusively Indian settlement anywhere in Manitoba.

Very recently we have begun to hear of First Nations and First Nations people. I believe the term developed among Indian people negotiating with government in recent land claims as a way of emphasizing that they descend from those who were here before the French and English. If the French and the English wish to style themselves the Founding Nations then why should bands of those who descend in significant measure from the people who were here before them not style themselves the First Nations? The term stretches the definition of nation but makes a point which needs acknowledgment.

I think First Nations people are best defined as those who perceive themselves as such on the basis of Indian ancestry of whatever degree. Its advantage is that it includes all aboriginal peoples, Indian and Inuit, Canadian and foreign. Its disadvantage is that it fails to resolve any of the ambiguities between aboriginal and part-aboriginal that some of the earlier terms distinguished. If the term is used integrally to a land claim settlement with government, it will require legal definition and may differ from the definition of status Indian under the Indian Act.

The term half-breed or breed, which, as I said above, was generally though not always a disrespectful term, is little heard now. At one time it was used commonly to refer to people of mixed ancestry who lived and worked in the non-Indian community and who, though they often would acknowledge their partial Indian ancestry, firmly avoided identity as Indians. Many were prone to be considerably offended if they were taken by strangers to be Indian or if people who did know them made incautious reference to their make-up. These people were numerous and often a majority in many non-Indian communities in rural Canada half a century ago.

We have some information about the numbers and distribution of people in Canada with Aboriginal ancestry.

The estimated population of Canadians at end of 1992 with Aboriginal origins was 980,500.

The status Indian population at the end of 1992 was 533,461.

The number of status Indians living on-reserve was 295,032.

The number of status Indians living on Crown land was 20,631.

The number of status Indians living off-reserve was 217,798.

Extrapolating from these numbers, there appear to be 447,000 people with Aboriginal origins but not with Indian status.

There is debate now between some Indian leaders and government about who should decide who is and is not an Indian and who should determine band membership.

The first point is perhaps more easily decided than the second.

The principle rationale for separate laws and programs for the people of mainly mixed ancestry whom we recognize as Indians is that because their descent was in significant measure from the people who were here when the Europeans first arrived, they are entitled to specific rights and benefits, often at a cost to public funds, not available to others.

There has to be a law, applicable across Canada, which determines who qualifies for these rights and benefits. While government should certainly consult with Indian leaders on the criteria to be enshrined in law, ultimately Parliament must make the law.

On the point of band membership, much of the benefit of Indian status is unattainable without membership in a band. There are a few such people, posted to a general list, but they have no right of residence on a reserve anywhere, no share in band funds nor in reserve-based resources.

Until recently, the government determined not only Indian status but band membership as well. Bands now may establish criteria for and control their own membership and may admit to membership persons without Indian status. Federal funding to bands to support reserve or crown land communities, however, is based on the resident membership of people with status.

There have been many instances over the years in which someone's perception of themselves as Indians, and the perception of other Indians that they are Indian, has not coincided with the provisions of the Indian Act. They have perceived themselves as Indian, the law has said the opposite.

Often this has led to life-long grievances, painful and irresolvable.

In other instances, the sense of Indian identity (irrespective of the degree of ancestry) has been so strong that what the law says is a matter of complete indifference.

Most painful of all have been cases in which people who perceive themselves to be Indians have been rejected by other Indians. Indian women who lost status on marriage to non-Indian men, under a provision of the Indian Act since amended, often found the loss painful; many have been further hurt when, on their reinstatement to Indian status, the leaders of their former bands have opposed their reinstatement to the band list.

A councilor of a band on the West Coast once complained about the number of people without status and of mixed ancestry, who, in his view, having for years denied or acknowledged as little as their possible Indian connections, were suddenly "coming out of the woodwork in droves" when the possibility of land claims benefits began receiving public attention. How might it have felt to have encountered this sentiment on making overtures to return to an Indian identity?

Given the extensive mixing of Indian people with Europeans, anomalies have been inevitable.

Most difficult for many Canadians to grasp is how far removed from the original inhabitants are the people who now hold Indian status.

Except in the most isolated bands, it is all but impossible to find anyone on a band list who is without mixed ancestry. Throughout the southern and eastern bands, the European influence in the ancestry is frequently predominant.

I grew up in a community in the Cariboo country of British Columbia in which a majority of people were of mixed ancestry but firmly not identifying as Indian and visibly not of full Indian ancestry. I also frequently met Indian people, either fully or predominantly of Indian ancestry, from bands which had remained substantially isolated and separate.

As a child, I thought the distinctions between Indians, part-Indians and white guys were straightforward and consistent.

Then in my early twenties I began working for the federal government in Indian programs. I worked out of Kamloops, and if I had not had access to the band lists I would have wondered why so many white guys and half-breeds (no offense intended) were living on the Indian reserves. In the light of my previous experience, the number of people of mixed ancestry on the band lists in which the European influence stood out unmistakably was nothing short of striking. Only older people on the lists, and not all of them, looked predominantly Indian.

I worked subsequently with bands throughout much of British Columbia and the Yukon Territory and I have met a number of Indians from other parts of Canada. I have seen photographs of Indian people in newspapers and magazines and in recent years I have seen many on television.

The sum of my experience over sixty years in Indian country is that people in Canada whom we call Indians are overwhelmingly people of mixed ancestry, many of them predominantly European.

To non-Indian Canadians of younger generations who have no experience of people with full or near full Indian ancestry, it is easy to assume that anyone who looks different from Europeans in the direction of Indian appearance is an Indian. Without reference to a band list, the many people with Indian status but without noticeable Indian appearance simply are not recognized as Indians.

In reality, not only is the ancestry among Indians already substantially mixed, it can only become more diluted as the generations go by. Looking different from Europeans will be increasingly less significant as an ingredient and indeed, many status Indians now cannot rely on their appearance as a marker.

If ancestry and physical appearance are increasingly less reliable as cornerstones of who they are, by what other means may we know them? How will we respect an identity that is increasingly difficult to recognize and, indeed, is increasingly variable as cultural dilution proceeds at differing rates, but inevitably, across the nation? How will we make sense of distinctions in law if we cannot make distinctions in fundamental identity?

The implications of a genetic shift toward increased European ancestry are difficult enough to grasp; the confusion following on cultural dilution can be horrendous.

I have known people barely recognizable, physically, as Indians who were culturally closer to pre-contact North American Indians than some others, visibly of Indian ancestry, who functioned in every respect in the wider society with no more grasp than any fully European or Asian Canadian of what it might mean to be Indian. Wanting to respect both, as you deal with the apparent white guy, you respect the fact that he perceives himself to be an Indian; as you deal with the apparent Indian, you respect the fact that he understands himself only as a white guy. If you imagine that somehow you can respect everyone by dealing with them as if they were all the same, you haven't spent much time in what these days is called a cross-cultural situation.

Even setting aside the striking difference in physical appearance and material culture, the Aboriginal North Americans were a profoundly distinct people from the arriving Europeans. Their languages, beliefs and customs were incomprehensibly different to the Europeans then and to those of us who might try to look back now in search of understanding.

Beliefs about the spirit world, about the relationship of mankind to the animals, land forms and water bodies, about kinship and kinship obligation, and about property were as close to being a world apart as could be imagined on the same planet.

The most extreme difference you might have found from one culture to another in the old world was nothing compared to the difference between any old world culture and pre-contact cultures prevailing in the new world.

Even today, an immigrant can come to Canada from virtually any of the regions in Europe and Asia familiar to Europeans five hundred years ago and move effortlessly, in a generation or less, into the wider Canadian society, a feat which continues to baffle great numbers of people, however mixed their ancestry, who descend from the original North Americans.

I once listened to a status Indian of about sixty, an hereditary and former elected chief of his band, try, with little success, to explain to a younger generation of elected band councilors, how different were the people who had been old when he was young.

I have forgotten the larger matter which made the issue important but I recall vividly how the older man kept repeating, in speaking of the old men who held the hereditary chieftain-ships when he was a boy, that they were a *different* people.

Significantly, he was not speaking of how different were the old chiefs from the Europeans then and now, but of how different they were from the Indian people of his generation and from the generation of the band leaders to whom he then spoke.

In the context, it was clear that the difference about which he spoke was the difference in beliefs and customs, in cultural values of every kind. He was, himself, visibly of mixed ancestry and the majority of the younger people to whom he spoke were indistinguishable, physically, from any European Canadians but this was a difference from the original people with which we were all so familiar we paid it no heed. His anxiety was to make it understood that this other difference, this profound differ-ence in culture, existed every bit as much.

Yet even those people of this younger generation who are as European in appearance as many a white neighbour in any non-native Canadian community perceive themselves to be different in some degree from other Canadians, a difference which derives, however distantly, from their ancestral links to the people who were here when their European forefathers arrived.

One may say, easily, in summary that First Nations or Abo-riginal or Indian people—choose your term—are of mixed ancestry and hybrid culture, different, as a group, from both their Aboriginal and their European forefathers and widely varying, as individuals, from each other; that they must live, by and large, within their own culture as they perceive it but as well within the wider Canadian society, a society defined by others. Significantly, they look to their Aboriginal ancestors, not their European, for their sense of who they are.

What that means, in practical application, is profoundly variable and perhaps impossible to grasp by anyone outside the fold.

For most if not all Aboriginal people, it means functioning in two cultures.

I have known many who function well in both. They have a strong sense of being Indian, whatever that might include in their particular case, and they deal effectively, with an obvious belief in their own worth, in the wider community. In many cases, these people communicate well in both their own language and in English, but not universally. I have known many people who are clearly comfortable with their Indian identity but cannot speak the language of their Aboriginal ancestors.

I have known many who have a difficult time in either culture. Often these are young people who find themselves unable to meet the expectations of the elders in their own community but who cannot, either, function satisfactorily in the non-native world. They receive negative messages about themselves wherever they go. In this situation, loss of language can be pivotal. Obliged to spend too much time in schools run by the dominant culture, they have not learned the language of their elders but neither have they become proficient in English.

Even among those who go confidently about in wider society, the supports of their own culture may remain critical in ways imperceptible to the outsider. A student who did very well in school and enjoyed a quiet popularity with her non-Indian classmates once told me how much she always wished to have at least one other Indian person somewhere in her vicinity. In a classroom full of white kids she would suffer a manageable but persistent unease beneath the surface; yet if she discovered there was another Indian student in the class next door, she could be entirely comfortable.

Ancestral imperatives mix frequently with today's business in the wider world. A few years ago, the elderly chief of a West Coast band wished to develop a strip of reserve land to generate revenue for the band's account. The opportunity was excellent and the old man's plan well thought out. With the new annual revenue, the band could generate other enterprises to employ band members and generally raise the level of economic opportunity and security for everyone.

The scheme was opposed by a former elected chief, a younger man, who successfully frustrated the older man's attempt to gain a majority support among the band members.

Both these men were hereditary chiefs of considerable significance; they were heir as well to incredibly convoluted feuds between clans and powerful families going back beyond memory. Neither had any idea how the trouble had begun but each devoted much of his life's energy to its perpetuation.

Neither displayed the least trace of their Indian ancestry in their physical appearance. The older man had blue eyes.

It is increasingly difficult for a non-Indian unfamiliar with the strength of this hybrid culture to understand that someone who looks white can actually be culturally someone else. I listened to a man of mixed ancestry try to convey this understanding to representatives of some commission or other who were visiting in the arctic community where he lived.

You have to understand, he explained, that we are a different people. You might think we are some kind of bush white man but we are not. We are a different people.

I found that simple statement particularly explicit because this man's father had been a bush white man. He had come into the country and adapted well. He had married a native woman and lived out his life with her people.

Their children, of which this man was one, had grown up with his mother's people. On another occasion he had explained to me how he had often fought with the other children as a boy because they had picked on him for being white. Still, he could only perceive himself as an Indian and to explain this to others, he fell on the distinction that he was not just some kind of bush white man.

It must be left to Indian people to convey, as they wish, what it means to be Indian, to be rooted culturally somewhere between the societies of their aboriginal ancestors and today's wider society. As that story is told, and here and there it has begun to be told, it will reveal a profoundly rich mix of highly variable experience: from that of the few remaining elders in remote regions who lived as children in a nomadic life only marginally removed from pre-contact society, to that of others, generations on, moving apace in the wider society, often with little about them to reveal their ancestral ties.

It will be a story of a cultural heritage richer than most non-Indian Canadians can possibly imagine without its telling, but a story as well of the ordinary and often too brutal human frailties which afflict us all.

Virtually universal in this story will be the pain of having been belittled, communally and individually, for generations by an insensitive and dominant society. To have it forced upon you, irrespective of any truth, that you are inferior, that your people are inferior, to be humiliated, to be reduced to beggary in your own land, to be stripped not only of power but of dignity as well—these are beyond the imagination of those of us who take for granted the accidents of birth which give us a place at the larger table.

White Europeans have been, until quite recently and virtually to the last man and woman, a blatantly racist lot. Even the well intended and essentially decent among us perceived others as lesser breeds, in need of care which only we, in our wisdom, could provide. The worst among us treated those not like us with mean and despicable cruelty.

Federal governments in Canada, by and large, though not always, have meant well by Indian people. Provincial and local governments have come to exhibit respect but historically they are better known for their bigotry. Ineptitude has figured more than malevolence in the federal government's contribution to the dismal side of Indian experience, the ineptitude often coupled with dreadful insensitivity in the public servants who carried out government policies and programs.

For sheer meanness, look to the bootlegger, the greedy storekeeper, the exploitative employer, the racist proprietor of a cafe, the arrogant neighbour and aggressive young white men in pursuit of sex and violence.

Treatment of Indians by police forces throughout Canada has been chequered.

Until recently, policing, particularly at the point of enforcement, lay in the hands of white men who took pride in being strong and tough. People who broke the law were a lesser lot, to be held in contempt, and none were lesser than Indians. Too often, individual police officers have welcomed the opportunity to use force, responding to spoken or physical resistance with rough treatment, on occasion with outright beatings.

That said, it is also the case that the majority of police officers have dealt reasonably with Indian people and in many communities, particularly in remote regions, mutual respect and trust have led to good relationships.

It is easy to pass judgment in hindsight but I am not at all sure that many of those who now condemn the treatment of Indian people in Canada by governments, institutions and individuals over the last half millennium would have managed much differently had they been in charge. This is not to say that wrongs have not been done—wrongs *have* been done—but to point out the difficulty of being altogether sure that what we do now will stand well in the judgment of posterity.

One could take the extreme position, which some do, that Europeans should never have settled, that when they discovered the New World, they should have had the decency to recognize it was already occupied and go home.

If the Europeans had resisted their desire to occupy the newly discovered lands, however, one certain consequence would be that today's First Nations people could never have lived, since virtually all descend in part from those immigrant races.

None of which is to say that today's Aboriginal people do not have legitimate grievances growing out of the historic relationship with the wider society, as well as painful difficulties living in modern Canada.

Tragically, there are large numbers of these people for whom the experience of being Indian in Canadian society has been and remains dismal, all too often helpless, a violent and miserable existence.

Clearly, the wider society owes these people whatever affordable and effective means can be found to alleviate their misery. Those means are elusive and it is not at all certain that present initiatives to settle land claims and establish self-government will be of much practical help, for example, to the sexually abused children now sniffing gasoline and sinking into suicide.

A danger in land claims settlements and self-government agreements is that these may enshrine in law differences between status Indians and other Canadians when real differences in race and culture are in fact diminishing.

When people's European ancestry predominates to the degree you can't tell they're Indian without the band list in hand, arguing they have an essential right to hunt or fish without restriction because they are status Indians is going to seem specious to say the least.

Settlement should be reached with the descendants of the Aboriginal people who were here when the Europeans arrived, but these settlements should take into account the fact that these claimants are also descended from the arriving Europeans whose taking of the land is held to be compensable.

(Paradoxically, many of the most effective negotiators on the Indian side in the land claims process are individuals obviously more European than Aboriginal.)

The task is enormously complex, but it is not at all unthinkable that a day will come when the only way of telling Indians from non-Indians is by the special treatment those with legal Indian status receive from government. When that happens, it will be better if those special treatments are not irreversible.